WESTWARD THE WILDERNESS

STONECROFT SAGA 3

B.N. RUNDELL

WOLFPACK
PUBLISHING
—— EST 2013 ——

WOLFPACK
PUBLISHING
— EST 2013 —

Westward The Wilderness

Paperback Edition
Copyright © 2020 B.N. Rundell

Wolfpack Publishing
6032 Wheat Penny Avenue
Las Vegas, NV 89122

wolfpackpublishing.com

Paperback ISBN 978-1-64734-305-7
eBook ISBN 978-1-64734-684-3

Library of Congress Control Number: 2020933620

WESTWARD THE WILDERNESS

1 / Departure

The long-legged black stallion stepped out, excited to be back on the trail. It had been a long winter, but the herd of mustangs held by the Osage had more than its share of mares that would not soon forget the Andalusian bred stallion. The beautiful sixteen hand stud had been purchased from a band of gypsies as they traveled through Eastern Pennsylvania with a stop at Philadelphia and the Stonecroft estate. The elder Stonecroft made the two-year old colt a present for his son who was to enter the university that fall and the two had been inseparable ever since. Gabriel Stonecroft, now known as Gabe Stone, and his life-long friend, Ezra Blackwell left Philadelphia one year ago this spring, with a pack of ne'er-do-well bounty hunters hot on their trail.

Gabe had become the focus of the bounty hunters when he killed the son of a prominent and wealthy merchant known only as Old Man Wilson. Old Man Wilson had been known for his penchant of stopping at nothing to accomplish his goals, whether in business, social or personal affairs. He had doted on his only son and repeatedly bailed him out of trouble, teaching the young man that wealth and rank had privileges and they were above the law. That attitude had given the young man the idea that he could do whatever he chose and would often make unwelcome advances toward the young women of Philadelphia society. It was one of those shunned advances that prompted Gabe to defend the honor of his sister and confront Jacob Wilson, which resulted in the duel. Gabe sought to spare the man's life, but when he refused to abide by the *Code Duello*, he had no choice but to shoot and his shot was lethal. Jacob Wilson's death resulted in the two friends leaving their homes and families to spare them the brokenhearted wrath of Old Man Wilson.

Now, after spending the fall and winter with the Osage people, Gabe and Ezra reluctantly departed the village of their friends to follow their long-held dream of exploring the wilderness west of the Mississippi River, the land of *La Louisiane* that had been ceded to the Spanish in 1763. Living in the seat of the young government of the colonies, Washington D.C., made Gabe privy to information that led him to understand that all the territory between the Mississippi River and the Pacific Ocean was land that the new government coveted and hoped to one day add to the young nation.

Gabe and Ezra had long talked about the wilderness and they shared the dream of one day exploring the unknown lands. This was a dream birthed in the woods of Pennsylvania when the two boys wandered, hunted and shared imaginations. They had always seen themselves as great adventurers, and the circumstances brought on by the duel had now made it possible. The friends rode silently, somewhat morose, as they hunched their shoulders to the morning chill and let the horses have their head. They would miss their friends and the comforts of the Osage camp.

It was just an hour's ride to the trading post of Choteau known as Fort Carondelet and the two-story structure came into sight just as the first grey light of morning pierced the shadows of the woods beside them. One man was swinging a double-bladed ax, splitting wood for their fires. Between swings, the movement from the trees caught his attention and he reached for the rifle leaning against the tree, but a hail from Gabe, "Ho! We're friendly, needin' supplies!" stopped the man.

Gabe couldn't blame the man for being a little skittish. Just last fall, shortly after the post was built, the post had been raided by some freebooters who killed all the traders and looted the post. The past winter had been good to them and Choteau's post had done well. Gabe and Ezra stepped down, tethering their horses at the hitching rail and asked, "Got'ny coffee on?"

"Oui! You bet!" answered the wood-splitter, burying the head of the axe in the stump and grabbing an armload of firewood. His pants legs were tucked in the top of his tall lace up boots and galluses stretched over his shoulders to hold the britches at a respectable height. A long-sleeved faded red union suit served to cover the mass of hair that sought escape above the last button by the man's neck. He had a pencil thin moustache that barely showed with his week's growth of whiskers darkening his face. Friendly eyes shone from under the thick eyebrows and a broad smile showed white teeth..

He pushed open the door with his foot, and spoke over his shoulder, "I am Jacques Minnard, and my partner," nodding his head toward the interior, "is John Smith, and he says he has no kin among the many Smiths that populate this great country!"

Gabe introduced himself and Ezra and asked, "So, how are you supplied after that raid by that bunch of crooks?" as they followed Jacques into the post.

"Oh, we are well supplied. When we," he motioned to his partner and himself, "came from St. Louie we brought several wagons of supplies. Those we did not keep went to the fort on the Verdigris. Now, what can we help you with, monsieur?"

"Well sir, we need some of just 'bout ev'r'thing. Staples, lead, powder, and such. But we also need some information," began Gabe, handing a list of needs to the trader. The man looked at the list, handed it to Smith and leaned on his elbows on the counter, "And just what kind of information?"

Gabe stood with one side at the counter, his arm outstretched and palm on the counter as he looked at Jacques and asked, "We're goin' west. I'm thinkin' the best way west is to go north to the Missouri River and follow it a spell. Maybe take the Platte River on west, or even the upper end of the Missouri. I was wonderin' what you might know as to the whereabouts of any other traders or about any routes west."

"*Oui, oui, m'sier, je comprends.* I have been in the posts of Choteau on the Missouri and I have heard others talk about the west. If you go north, before the Missouri bends to the north, there is a post among the Otoe or Missouria Indians. It is a post of Choteau. I have heard others speak of a new fort farther north, above the mouth of the Platte, put in by James Mackey. And there is talk of another even further upstream well past the confluence with the Niobrara river, but I do not know if that one is there or not."

"And what about the Indians? What tribes and are they friendly?"

Jacques stood upright, leaned on the counter and showing a broad smile, "*Ah, difficile á savoir,* ze Indians, so many and so different. Friendly today, enemy tomorrow. The Otoe and Missouria near the Choteau post, they are friendly. But the Sioux and Pawnee, who knows?"

Gabe looked at Ezra and back at Jacques, "Then if you worked at the Choteau post among 'em, put together some trade goods they might like and add it to the stack."

"*Oui, oui.* Most Indians want to trade for muskets, should I include some?"

"Yes, put four on the stack, add molds, lead and powder, and call it good."

By just a little past mid-morning, they were back on the trail, and Ezra asked, "So, tell me again how we're going west but traveling north?"

Gabe chuckled, "While I was at the university, as you know, I did considerable study of what is known as the western lands. There have been expeditions by the Spaniards going back as far as early the fifteen hundreds, Coronado, de Vaca, Cabrillo, and others, but most of their explorations are in the south. Now in the north, there have been forays by the French, but one fable always fascinated me, about the lost brethren of the Welsh. Supposedly a light-skinned people that speak some words that sound Welsh and have lighter colored hair are thought to be descendants of Prince Madoc and his followers that were rumored to have emigrated around 1170. There are also those that believe those same people are actually descendants of Norsemen."

"Welsh and Norsemen? If that don't beat all!" answered Ezra, shaking his head.

"Ummmhummm, I know. However, since we're in the neighborhood . . ."

"Neighborhood? And just how far north is this 'neighborhood?'" asked Ezra, skeptically.

"Well, according to Jacques, a week, ten days, maybe more. But, if we see a likely looking route that beckons, there's nothing that says we can't take it!" suggested Gabe.

The men fell silent, contemplative, considering, until Ezra spoke, "Norsemen, Welsh, French traders and missionaries, Spaniards exploring and trading, add in all the Indians and just what is it that we're gonna be exploring that hasn't already been seen by all these?"

Gabe chuckled, "It seems to me I've heard you quote the Bible where it says 'there is no new thing under the sun.'"

"And all this time I had visions of us standing where no man had ever stood before. High up on some mountain top, overlooking our vast domain, and thinking we would be the first men to see it." He turned in his saddle, one hand on the pommel and the other on the cantle, looking at Gabe, "You sir, have shattered my dream!"

Gabe reined up and turned to look at his friend. He stretched out one arm, made a sweeping motion before them, "Tell me, dreamer, how many people do you see?"

Ezra frowned, looked in the direction they traveled, "Why, none."

"And this is just a few days west of the Mississippi, and you see no one. And when we were with the Osage on the buffalo hunt, how many people, other than the Osage, did you see?"

Ezra nodded his head, "Again, I say none."

"And don't you think that the further north and west we travel, the land will be even less populous than what we've seen?"

"I certainly hope so! Still, with all those people you spoke about, don't you think we'll bump into some?"

"Perhaps a few, hopefully we'll find other traders as we need. I am certain we will pass many a day that we do not see another living person and when we get to those mountains, I would also believe we will find many a place that has never seen the passage of man."

Gabe nudged the big black forward, leading the way as he trailed the sorrel pack horse. Ezra kicked his bay alongside Gabe and said, "The first place we find like that, I'm gonna build me a cabin and stay right there!"

"Oh, you are, are you? Why?"

"Cuz that's where I wanna be, where there ain't nobody else."

"But Ezra, wherever you are, there you'll be, and it will no longer be a place where there is nobody, because you'll be there."

Ezra scowled, looked at his friend, "Oh, yeah. You're right." He paused, thinking, "But, there won't be anybody else!"

"Not unless you find another Indian woman that thinks you're a good candidate for a husband! You know, like Grey Fox of the Osage. For a while there, I thought you'd be stayin' behind with her."

Ezra's shoulders slumped and he hung his head, and answered just above a whisper, "For a while there, I thought so too."

They rode quietly, remembering their time with the Osage and the women that had become so special to them. It had been very tempting to stay, for the villagers had become their friends and they would have been welcomed, but there was always the possibility of Old Man Wilson upping the bounty and more freebooters being tempted to come into the wilderness after the reward. The people of the village would feel honor-bound to join the fight as they had done before, but neither Gabe nor Ezra wanted any of their Osage friends to be harmed because of the evil deeds of a vengeful man, and so they chose to leave and continue their journey to the west in fulfillment of their life-long dream.

Gabe broke the reverie when he pointed with his chin, "Looks like we got us a river to cross." He lifted his eyes to the sky, "It'll be dusk soon, we've got plenty of time. We can cross over and make camp on the other side. Maybe you can get us some fresh meat."

Ezra pointed to their left, "We gonna cross that crick, an' then the river? Or we gonna do it all to onct an' cross below there," nodding his head to the bigger stream.

"Let's take a closer look-see," proposed Gabe, turning the black toward the riverbank.

As they looked at the murky and slow-moving water, Gabe said, "I think it'll be just as easy to cross here." He pointed across the river that was about seventy-five feet wide, "looks like a decent campsite on the sandbank there."

"Or up above there, in the trees. Might be more grass for the horses."

The crossing proved to be easy, good gravel bottom and water barely deep enough to get the horses' bellies wet. Ezra's choice of a campsite proved to be the best and Gabe offered to get the camp and fire ready as Ezra started toward the brushy riverbank in hopes of bagging a deer for their supper.

Gabe rubbed all the horses down with handfuls of grass, tethered them where they could reach ample graze, and with all the gear stacked under the trees, he started the fire for the evening. He gathered an armload of dry wood and positioned the fire under the long reaching branches of a big oak, knowing the new buds and leaves would dissipate the smoke as it rose. Gabe and Ezra had learned that as they traveled they should gather any edibles that were readily available. At the edge of the river Gabe found some fresh shoots of cattail and cut a hat full to add to the fresh deer meat that would be fried in the bear fat from the bear taken last fall while with the Osage.

Ezra soon returned, triumphant, with a young buck across his broad shoulders and grinning ear to ear. Gabe greeted him with, "Looks like a nice one. Bet he'll be nice and tender! I'll get things started while you slice us some steaks from the backstrap."

Ezra answered, "You know, I kinda like this arrangement, you know, you cookin' an' me huntin'."

"Don't let it go to your head my friend. That's only cuz we ain't in enemy territory. From what Jacques said, any Indians we run into 'tween here an' the Missouri River are mostly friendly. So, it didn't hurt for you to shoot that Lancaster rifle of yours. Otherwise, I hafta do the huntin' with my bow."

"I know, I know, but still . . ." he moaned, "I'll just enjoy it while I can."

2 / Missouria

The low rolling hills interspersed with grass covered flat-lands offered few trails other than the occasional game trail. The early start on the day's travel had given the two friends ample time on the move, but the thick woods often made the journey slow going. Gabe sat back, looking at the trees, trying to identify the variety of hardwoods and others. He especially enjoyed the dogwoods bringing forth the sweet-smelling white flowers and the redbud with its bright purple blossoms that gave the woods a variety of colors only seen in the springtime. The tall elm and oak seemed to anchor the forest while the smaller ash, walnut and cypress offered shade and homes to the many forest creatures, most of who chattered warnings to the passersby.

It was a good day to travel, the sky was void of clouds, the air was springtime cool, and the horses were glad to be on the trail and stepped out to a lively gait, heads bobbing, ears forward, and often found the game trails before their riders. They kicked a few deer out of their beds, sent some rabbits and squirrels scampering, and heard the alarm cries of circling hawks. The world was alive with the newness of spring and they enjoyed an occasional glimpse of a spotted fawn trying its legs for its first steps, or a black bear cub taking a tumble down a hillside.

After their mid-day break and brief rest, they were again on the move, making the best of the good weather.

As the long branches of the tall timber cradled the sun, just long enough for old sol to paint the sky with its muted shades of gold and orange, the two friends searched for a clearing with nearby water for their night's stop. They were about to break from the timber when Gabe reined up, holding his hand up to stop Ezra. He motioned his friend forward and to his side and stood in his stirrups to scan beyond the trees. "I don't like it. The hair on my neck is tellin' me somethin's wrong, and Ebony's ears haven't stopped twitching."

Ezra quietly stepped down, rifle in hand and slowly walked forward, using the trees for cover. He froze in place, one foot lifted, then slowly lowered it into the tall grass. He lowered himself to one knee, while motioning for Gabe to join him. They were on a slight rise, overlooking a grassy meadow that bordered a small winding river. In the grassy flats, over three hundred yards distant, a band of Indians were making their camp. Most were erecting lean-tos, others tending horses, some bringing firewood, and many women busy making ready to cook a meal. Several warriors, still horseback, came from the trees and many rode horses with fresh-killed deer draped over their haunches.

"What tribe you reckon they are?" asked Ezra, watching the activity of the people.

"Dunno, for sure, but this area's s'posed to be Missouria country."

"They friendly?" asked Ezra.

"S'posed to be but can't never tell." Gabe looked to his friend, "Why, you plannin' on invitin' 'em to supper?"

"Humph, no, but I wouldn't mind gettin' an invitation. 'Sides, ain't we supposed to be neighborly an' introduce ourselves?"

"What if they decide to have *you* for supper?" asked Gabe, chuckling.

"Hah! You know Indians don't like dark meat! You're the one that should be skeered, cuz I did hear that most of these natives kinda hanker to white meat!"

Gabe looked at his friend, laughed, and stood up to return to his horse. "Well, come on! If we're gonna be neighborly. Tain't polite to wait till the last minute when all the work is done."

As they rode from the trees, they were side-by-side, both men holding their reins in one hand, the other on their thigh, near the holster of their saddle pistol. They were immediately spotted by the warriors and several turned their mounts to face the intruders. Gabe raised his hand and spoke loudly, "Aho!"

Three warriors started their horses toward the two men that approached their camp, spread out to block the way.

The man in the middle raised his open hand and answered, "Aho."

Using sign language, Gabe asked if they spoke any language of the white men. The leader answered no, then asked if Gabe spoke any language of the natives. Gabe grinned, spoke some words in Osage, until the man, after chuckling a little spoke in English. "I know your language. I learned from traders of the British. Who are you and why are you here in our land?"

"I am Gabe, this is Ezra, and we're just passing through. Going north and west to the far mountains. Who are you and your people?"

"We are *Niúachi* but there are those that call us Missouria. You spoke words of the Osage; do you know them?"

"Yes, we wintered with Blue Corn's people. But you never told me your name," said Gabe, waiting.

"I am Strong Bull. Our people are going to the west for our buffalo hunt." He leaned to the side to look at the heavy-laden pack horses and asked, "You have come to trade?"

"We can trade, we have some goods you might like," answered Gabe, glancing at Ezra.

"Then you are welcome to our village. We will eat, and then we will trade," said Strong Bull, reining his horse around and motioning for Gabe and Ezra to follow.

Lame Deer and Fawn of the Morning, Strong Bull's woman and daughter, prepared a sumptuous meal of deer meat, given by Ezra, and squash and beans from their dried winter stores. Strong Bull was anxious to get the trading started, as he had eyed the trade rifles on Gabe's packhorse. But Strong Bull had little that Gabe wanted, but after much bickering and including two other couples of the band, Gabe settled for two sets of buckskins, a pair of high-topped beaded moccasins, and a beaded possibles bag, and Strong Bull had his rifle and accouterments. Because the Missouria wore breech cloths and leggings, they would have to wait another day for the women to finish the buckskin britches, one set for each of them. The Missouria had planned on staying in this camp for another day, it would be a good opportunity for Gabe and Ezra to learn more about these people.

Gabe and Ezra stood as Gabe said, "We will make our camp there in the trees across the water," pointing with his chin. "Send someone over with word when the work is done."

Strong Bull stood, holding his new rifle with pride. He looked at Gabe, smiling, "I will have Fawn of the Morning bring them to you. She and her mother will make them special for you." At his word, Lame deer held a tunic across the shoulders of Gabe, then with a piece of cord measured him for a proper fit of the britches. Fawn of the Morning, a young woman of about thirteen summers, did the same for Ezra. The women stepped away, spoke to Strong Bull in their language and Bull said to Gabe, "After the mid-day meal." Gabe and Ezra shook hands with Bull and went to their horses to go to their camp.

As they prepared their camp at the edge of the trees just back from the thick brush at the bank of the river, Ezra spoke, "You let Bull have that rifle a mite cheap, didn't you?" Gabe chuckled as he stripped the gear from the pack horses, "Yeah, but we made a friend and that can be more valuable than anything."

Ezra, wiping down his bay with a handful of grass, replied, "Yeah, s'pose you're right. But I was hopin' to get me a set of moccasins, mine're gettin' a mite thin."

"Well, we'll go back over a little early and maybe we can do some more tradin' and get you some."

The men had been asleep for a good while when Gabe suddenly came awake. He moved only his eyes, listening and looking for he knew something had awakened him. He heard Ebony stomp his feet and snort and Gabe glanced his way to see the big stallion, head up, eyes wide and ears pricked, looking towards the river. Gabe slowly moved his head to look, grasping his belt pistol in his left hand and feeling for his Ferguson rifle with the other. The dim light from the stars and half-moon in the clear night gave him a good view of the meadow beyond the stream and everything looked quiet.

He sat up slowly, looking again at Ebony who still showed alarm. He stealthily got to his feet, stuffed the pistol back in his belt, slipped the possibles bag and powder horn over his shoulder and lifted the Ferguson, muzzle down and butt at his shoulder. He quietly brought it to full cock as he searched the trees nearby and across the river. A whisper came from Ezra, "What is it?"

"Dunno," answered Gabe, also in a whisper. Ezra was at his side, rifle in hand, as they stepped behind trees nearer the water.

"There! To the right at the trees!" came the whispered warning from Ezra.

Gabe looked as directed and movement showed in the moonlight. Several warriors were crawling through the tall grass toward the village. Gabe glanced at the moon, then to the eastern sky, and realized these attackers were unable to be seen from the village and were getting into position to attack the village at first light. "We've got to warn them!"

"How?" asked Ezra.

Gabe nodded and began backing away from the river and into the thicker trees. He looked at Ezra, "Think you can cross over downstream and come back to Bull's camp and not be seen?"

"Yeah, but what about you?"

"I think I can do more damage if I catch 'em from behind, keep 'em from getting away. If I cross over there," pointing upstream toward the trees beyond the clearing, "maybe I can get to their horses. Then hit 'em from behind and we'll catch 'em 'tween us."

Ezra nodded and said, "I'll get my saddle pistol too. It's a good thing that river ain't more'n a crick and not but knee deep. I just hope I don't get my head shot off by some of Bull's warriors."

"You can do it. You're better in the woods than anybody, including me!"

When Ezra came from the water, he stood quietly, looking through the thin brush and trees for any sign of a lookout. He moved in a crouch, measuring each step carefully, watching through the dim light for any sign of alarm. He started to move past a big oak, when he heard movement, something brushing the bark of the tree, and froze. One warrior, a young buck, leaned against the tree using a lance to steady himself as his head drooped. Ezra waited till the lookout stood still, then stepped around the tree and put his hand over the man's mouth and his forearm pushing him tight against the tree. He whispered, "I'm here to warn you! Stand easy!" He didn't know if the young warrior understood his words, but he understood his strength as he fought for breath under the pressing arm. Ezra slowly removed his hand from the man's mouth, and said, "There are warriors coming through the grass, yonder!" pointing with his chin, "We have to warn Strong Bull!" He repeated Bull's name in Spanish, hoping the young man understood. When the warrior nodded his head, Ezra stepped back and whispered, "Let's go!" and followed the lookout to the lean-to of Strong Bull.

Their presence alerted Bull at their approach and he sat up, reaching for his new rifle. He recognized Ezra and started to speak but was stopped at Ezra's hand signal. He knelt beside the leader and whispered, pointing toward the grasses. "There are many warriors nearing your camp. They do not know they were seen; we saw from our camp. If they see movement, they will know they are seen. Can you warn your people?" Bull nodded and rolled from his blankets.

Gabe was loaded down with hardware. Two saddle pistols, the French made over-under double barreled matched pair that were the pride of his father, and his turn-over double-barreled Bailes belt pistol. The French pistols had dual locks and triggers, but the turn-over was as the name implied, had one lock and the barrels had to be turned before firing again. His Ferguson rifle cradled in his arm, he moved through the river, letting the chuckling of the low water cover the sound of his movements. When he had left home, his father, who had been an avid collector, outfitted him with the best weapons available, and the Ferguson rifle was a rarity with its breech-loading mechanism that allowed Gabe to easily load and fire as often as seven times a minute. While an experienced rifleman could load and fire his muzzle-loading flintlock two or three times in a minute, the Ferguson made Gabe equal to two or three men. With the added firepower of the pistols, he could get off seven shots in his first volley, enough to give any attackers second thoughts.

In his first summer out of Philadelphia, he and Ezra had been put to the test time and again when their flatboat was attacked by river pirates. Now proven in battle, the two men were confident in their ability to rout most attackers. Gabe had passing thoughts of those previous fights and knew it was good to learn from each conflict, and the two men had done just that, often reviewing each fight on what they was successful and what lessons they had learned from mistakes.

Now Gabe stepped onto the sandbar at the edge of the water and dropped to one knee, searching the trees at the creekside and beyond.

Gabe moved as quiet as the early morning breeze, careful to choose his next step and move to another tree, all the while looking for the horses of the attackers. He paused, scrutinized the trees and examined the terrain, thinking about the best location for hiding the horses, knowing they would be far enough from the clearing to avoid scenting the horses from Strong Bull's camp and nickering a greeting. He saw what appeared to be a brushy depression, then lifted his eyes to the sky, judging his time until the first light that would signal the attack.

With a deep breath that lifted his shoulders, he dropped to his knees, cradling his rifle in his elbows and moved closer to the depression. He heard the stomping of hooves and an occasional snort and knew he had found the horses. The area was a dry creek bed, marked by a flat stone face along the near side where a lone guard sat, leaning back and dozing. Gabe slowly inched closer. He lay aside his rifle, took the two saddle pistols from his belt and lay them beside the rifle. He drew his Flemish made knife and crawled to the edge of the cliff. He slowly stood, careful to not alarm the horses, and with one long step, came to the side of the guard. He thrust his left hand over the man's mouth and drew the knife blade across his throat as he stared into the wide eyes of the guard. A gurgle came from the man as he struggled, but Gabe held his head against the cliff face until he quit moving, then slowly lowered his body to the ground.

The smell of blood and the rustle of movement caused the horses to snort and side-step, but Gabe spoke softly before he moved to calm the animals. They had been picketed to a long braided rawhide rope, and Gabe went to each lead line, cut it, and when all the horses, fifteen in all, had been freed, he jumped and waved, slapping them on the necks and rumps to scatter them into the trees. Satisfied, he retrieved his weapons and started back to the meadow. The attack would begin soon, and if Ezra had warned them, these attackers were in for a surprise.

3 / Fight

Word spread quickly and silently throughout the encampment of the Missouria. Bull said they had over thirty warriors, "And many of the women are proven fighters," he added as he and Ezra took their position near the lean-to. His wife and daughter had been instructed to stay in the cover of the lean-to and to stay low. After the attack, if it was best, they would make their way to the stream and cross over, but for now, so as not to warn the attackers, they would remain.

A quick glance to the east told Ezra of the coming dawn, the thin grey line that was the precursor of morning's light made dim shadows of the distant rolling hills. He looked to Bull who had also taken a quick glance to the east and nodded his head as they readied themselves. Ezra noticed the glee that showed in Bull's eyes as he thought about using his new rifle in the coming battle and remembered his own anticipation and fear when he and Gabe faced their first real fight against a band of renegade Shawnee. Ezra had been blooded in battle and now it was an experienced, although wary, warrior who awaited the attack.

The two-tone whistle of a meadowlark came from the tall grass. It was too early for the usual birdcall, and knowing the attackers were in the grass, it was the only warning for the Missouria. Instantly the attacking warriors rose and sent a volley of arrows arching into the camp. It was followed by the screams and war-cries as they started running toward the camp, anticipating their attack being a total surprise. The leaders of the charge made no more than two lunging steps before a barrage of rifle fire sounded from the shadowy camp and a hail of bullets took their toll. The smoke from the rifle fire masked much of the camp, but other warriors sent arrows at those that had yet to be hit.

Bull's first shot surprised him as much as the others when the rifle bucked and roared as it spat its cloud of smoke. He scrambled to reload, but his inexperience brought confusion and fear to his face as he snatched a fearful look toward the attackers. Ezra's first shot had scored, and a screaming warrior swallowed a ball of lead as he tumbled over backwards into the tall grass. But the others kept coming and one warrior, bare-chested, a porcupine roach in his hair and feathers fluttering behind, raised his gunstock war club overhead to strike Bull. Ezra snatched his pistol from his belt, cocking it as it came up and triggered a shot that took the warrior in his breastbone, sapping the strength in his arms and legs as he crumpled to the ground at Bull's feet.

The Missouria chief looked at Ezra, then back to his rifle to finish reloading, energized by the attack. He quickly raised his rifle towards another attacker and fired. But in his haste, he had forgotten to remove the ramrod and the lead ball pushed it out of the muzzle and into the belly of a Pawnee attacker. Bull brought the rifle back down to reload, but once the powder had been put into the muzzle and the patched ball placed and prodded, he reached for the ramrod feeling only the empty slot and ferrules. He looked around, then realizing what happened, he glanced at Ezra and caught the thrown ramrod from him. With a quick nod, he rammed his ball home, tossed the rod to Ezra and searched for another target, but the remaining attackers were running away through the tall grass.

Of the fifteen Pawnee, Gabe had taken the horse guard, and in the attack the Missouria had downed nine more. One of those retreating was wounded and dragged a bloody leg, trying to keep up with the others that were fleeing to the horses. Suddenly a blast came from the tree-line and one man tumbled into the grass face first. Another cloud of smoke and the roar of a shot came from near the same spot and caught another of the Pawnee. The remaining attackers dropped into the grass, scattering apart. There was shouting among the four, trying to decide and one took command and shouted for them to scatter and charge at his word.

Within moments, one man screamed his war cry and rose up, prompting the others to join in the attack on the shooters in the tree line. Their pause had given Gabe time to reload both his rifle and pistol, and the leader did not have time to take more than two steps nor finish his war cry when the .65 caliber ball from the Ferguson rifle took him in the face and blasted out the back of his skull. Before the others could react, Gabe brought up his saddle pistol, fired both barrels at two men who were shoulder to shoulder and both men spun around, dropping to the ground.

Two warriors remained, one already dragging a wounded leg, and both went to the grass. As Gabe watched the grass moving, he reloaded his Ferguson, waiting for any possible shot. He hollered at the men in the grass, "I can kill you easy! You don't have to die! Stand up!" He repeated his warning in Spanish and waited just a moment. The grass moved slightly, but no one stood. Gabe knew it wouldn't be smart to go into the grass after the man or men, and he waited. Once again, he shouted a warning, but no one stood. He brought the rifle to bear on the last movement of the grass, waited, and at the slightest movement, he fired. The big rifle roared and spat smoke and death, and the unmistakable thump of ball hitting flesh was heard instantly followed by a grunt and slight squeal that reminded Gabe of the sound the pigs had made art butchering day. Death has a way of making all creatures equal.

Gabe watched the grass as he reloaded once again, waiting, unsure if there were more. Then he saw a hand raise, "Alright, stand if you can," he said, lifting the rifle to cover the warrior. Slowly a man stood, stumbled a little and looked at Gabe with fear in his eyes. Both hands were raised shoulder high and both had blood on them. Gabe asked, "Are there others?" He received only a confused look and a shrug of shoulders from the man, indicating to Gabe he did not understand. He motioned to the man to come forward and he slowly stumbled toward the trees. Using sign, Gabe again asked if there were others and was answered with a hanging head shaken side to side showing both a negative answer and sorrow at the loss of his friends.

Gabe motioned for him to sit at the base of a tree, then set aside his rifle and knelt to take a look at the wound. The hole went completely through in the lower thigh. Although bleeding, Gabe was certain it would not be fatal. But now, what to do with him?

Gabe grabbed some moss from the back of the tree that supported the wounded man, cut some strips from his breechcloth, much to the dismay of the wounded man, and after wiping the wound as clean as possible, he used the moss and the strips to make a bandage to stay the blood. He used sign to tell the man the horses were gone, and for him to stay where he was while he went back to the Missouria camp. "I will come back soon," he said, using sign to make sure the man understood. With a nod of his head, his captive agreed and leaned back against the tree. Gabe picked up his rifle and stood, taking a quick look at the man, then started for the camp.

As he neared the camp, he saw several Missouria warriors stripping the bodies of the Pawnee and some were mutilating them. He turned away to look for Ezra, spotted him by the lean-to of Strong Bull and quickly made his way to their side.

Bull smiled broadly and said, "You two saved our people! We are grateful! How can we ever repay you?"

He turned slightly to point to the far tree-line, "There's a wounded Pawnee yonder. I don't know what you want to do with him, but . . ." he looked back at Bull to see a stern frown.

"Why did you not kill him?" he growled.

"He was already wounded and couldn't fight anymore. Didn't see no need to kill him."

Bull looked at Gabe as if there was something wrong with him. "But you killed many others."

"Well, yeah, but they were trying to kill me or my friends. That man had given up and couldn't kill anybody," explained Gabe, concerned.

Bull looked away, saw a warrior returning from his deeds in the grass and motioned him over. He looked to Gabe, "I will send this man to kill the Pawnee."

Gabe held up his hand, "Whoa now, wait on that. He's my prisoner, right?"

"Yes, he is yours. Do you not want him dead?" asked Bull, showing his confusion.

"No," answered Gabe, glancing at Ezra with a quick wink, "We'll keep him, make him our slave."

Bull grinned, nodding his head, "Good, good. It is good to have a slave to do your work."

Gabe looked at the chief, "Also Bull, I scattered the horses of that bunch. There's about fifteen of 'em runnin' loose in the woods if you want your men to gather them up."

Bull nodded, sent the summoned man to tell the others,

and turned to Gabe. "You have done much for our people. We will not forget this."

"Well, right now, we'll go back to our camp and pack up. As soon as those buckskins are done, send Fawn of the Morning over with 'em and we'll be on our way."

"It is good," answered Strong Bull.

4 / Captive

"So, what're we gonna do with him? Surely, you're not serious about making him a slave?" asked Ezra, incredulously, looking at the young Pawnee sitting against the tree.

Gabe chuckled, looked at his friend, "No, but I figgered that was the only way to get him away from here alive. I'm thinkin' he can travel with us a spell, at least till we get near his people. Then, we let him loose, or take him back and make friends, or . . ." shrugging his shoulders.

"Friends? With the Pawnee? After what we've done? And I don't mean just here. If you remember we had a run-in with them last fall with the Osage, and some of 'em survived and might remember us!" declared Ezra.

"Well, we'll just take it one day at a time, whatsay? Until then, he'll need somethin' to ride so while you help him back to our camp, I'll go get him a horse from those that I spooked off."

"Help him? And what if he tries to cut my throat or take

my scalp or sumpin'?"

Gabe looked at the Pawnee and using sign, told him what they would do, warned him to not try anything or this man whose skin was as the darkest night, would send him to his ancestors. Then he asked his name. He responded, "I have never seen a man with night skin, and my name is Night Wolf."

Gabe chuckled, looked at Ezra, knowing he was as fluent with sign as himself and asked, "Ain't that something, oh man whose skin is as the darkest night?"

"Where'd you come up with that? 'Sides, my skin ain't that dark. More like dusk than midnight," he responded, looking at his arm and back to Gabe.

Both men laughed and Gabe said, "Just get him to camp. I'll be back shortly, I hope."

Ezra had the fire going, coffee perking, and meat sizzling when Gabe returned riding a steel-dust gelding that brought a smile to the captive's face. Gabe noticed his response and asked, "Was this your horse?"

Night Wolf struggled to his feet, reaching toward the horse and nodded his head. It was obvious the two knew each other as the man stroked the horse's muzzle and the animal pushed his head against the man. "He hadn't gone far and trailing his lead like he was, he was easy to catch," said Gabe, using sign as he spoke. He slipped from the horse, handed the lead to Night Wolf and stepped to the fire to pour himself some coffee. When Wolf turned toward Gabe, smiling, he signed, "What will you do now?"

"We're taking you with us until your leg heals up, then we'll probably take you to your people."

"Why would you do that? We are enemies," he asked.

"We are not enemies; I fought your people because they were attacking my friends. If you had not attacked, we could be friends."

"You will let me go?" he asked again.

"Yes, but you need to heal up. So, sit down, I need to change that bandage," instructed Gabe, motioning toward his leg and the nearby log.

On his return to camp, Gabe had spotted some poplar and gathered some inner bark, a hat full of the red sappy buds, and some of the leaves. Now he made a poultice of the combination and readied a new bandage of moss and buckskin. Wolf signed, "Are you a medicine man among your people?"

Gabe chuckled, answered, "No, I just know of this from the time spent with the Osage."

Wolf frowned, "You lived with the Osage?"

"Just spent the winter with them."

"A war party of my people went against the Osage in the time of colors. Many were killed and they spoke of a white man and a black man that fought with them. Was that you?"

Gabe breathed deeply, applied the bandage and tied it tightly, then sat back and looked at the captive. He answered, "Yes, that was us. We fought with our friends to protect their people."

Wolf sat quietly for a moment, looked up at Gabe, "You,"

nodding to Ezra also, "have shown yourselves to be great warriors. Many of my people have died at your hands."

"They too were great warriors," answered Gabe. "But in battle, we fight to live and to keep our friends alive. We do not think of the Pawnee as our enemy."

"Why did you not kill me when I stood in the grass?" asked Wolf.

"There is no honor in killing a wounded warrior. I could have killed you, but I chose not to, instead we will try to be your friend. But tell me, why do your people attack the Osage and the Missouria?"

Wolf struggled to sit up and once comfortable, began, "In the time of colors, our shaman or the keeper of the Morning Star bundle, had a vision to do the ceremony of the Morning Star. Our people have had two summers of poor harvest and the ceremony is to appeal to the Evening Star, the source of all animal and plant life, for a good harvest. To do that, we have to capture a young woman of another tribe. She is treated with great honor and respect and is offered to become the Evening star. When she is sacrificed, it is the mating of Evening Star and Morning Star and her blood will enter the earth and make the ground fertile to bring forth life. If we do not do this, my people will not have a good harvest, and many will die."

Gabe and Ezra had paid close attention to the signing of the man and now, understanding, shook their heads at the simplicity of their thinking and the sincerity of their purpose. Although wrong by the standards of Christianity

and the Scriptures, this long-held tradition had been no
different than that of many peoples around the world that
served false gods and believed sacrifices were necessary to
appease the gods or to gain favor with them. Gabe looked at
Wolf, dropped his head and then looked back at the man and
signed, "Many of your warriors have died and what about
their deaths? Are they not as important as the possible deaths
from a poor harvest?"

"What you have done is the same. You would give your
life to save those that are your friends, would you not do
more for those of your own family or people? We did not
come to kill, but to save our own people."

Gabe stood and walked away; he needed some time to di-
gest what he had just learned. There was no question that he
knew that human sacrifice was wrong, and he would always
fight to prevent it, but to question the motives of those that
only sought to save their own people, disillusioned though
they were, was another thing indeed.

It was late afternoon the following day when they rode up
to the trading post known as Choteau's post, situated on
the bank of the Missouri near the mouth of the Kaw River.
It was a sturdy stone structure much like the post near the
Osage, two stories with shooting ports in the floor of the second story and in each of the shuttered windows. There were
several horses tethered at one of the two hitching rails and
Gabe and Ezra used the other. After getting a suspicious look
from two men, obviously French *coureurs des bois* or early

trappers, Ezra chose to stay with the horses and the Pawnee while Gabe went into the post. Although it was unusual to see French trappers this far to the southwest from their usual grounds, they were easily recognized by their attire and constant stream of French accompanied by very animated gestures. Though Ezra and Gabe were not interested in trapping and would not be any competition for the men and their pelts, they elicited great suspicion from the men.

One of the men gave a sidelong glance to Ezra, then spoke to his friend. They paused, looked again, then approached. One man asked in broken English, "Monsieur, are you a slave?"

Ezra dropped his head, shaking it side to side, then looked up at the men grinning, "No sir, I am not, nor have I ever been a slave. I am, like my friend," nodding toward the post, "free born."

They nodded, smiling, then asked, "And the Indian? He is your slave?"

Again Ezra chuckled, smiling, and answered, "No, he is not our slave. He was wounded and we are taking him back to his people."

"Would you sell him to us? We could use a slave to help with our pelts."

"Sell him?! No! I said, he's not a slave."

"But, monsieur, our people to the north have many such slaves. He is *Panis,* is he not?"

Ezra scowled, recognized the pronunciation of the word as sounding like what he knew and answered, "He is of the

Pawnee people, yes."

Both of the French men nodded, smiling, "Ah, I thought so. There are as many *Panis* as Negroes that are slaves in French Canada. Are you sure you will not sell him?"

Ezra suddenly drew his saddle pistol, cocking it as he brought it up to lay across his pommel, "You're getting me upset. I suggest you leave and leave in a hurry before I send you to French Canada in a box!"

The men were startled, but one man said, "You only have one shot, there are two of us!"

"Look at the end of this pistol. Now, how many barrels do you see?" snarled Ezra.

The men stared, looked up at the scowling face of Ezra and hurriedly unhitched their horses and mounted up to leave. With nothing more than a glance over their shoulders at Ezra, they kicked their horses to a gallop and disappeared into the trees and brush at the river's edge. Ezra shook his head and mumbled as he holstered the pistol with a glance at a smiling Wolf.

He said, "If only you could understand what they said."

Ezra stepped down, motioned for Wolf to do the same and the two men stretched their legs as they waited for Gabe. Although they needed little in the way of supplies, they never passed up an opportunity to garner any information about the country and people. In a short while, Gabe came from the post, smiling and looked at Ezra, seeing he was a little upset. He asked, "So, what's got under your skin, my friend?"

"Did you see those two Frenchies that came out just as

you went in?"

"Yeah, what about them?" asked Gabe, leaning against the hitchrail.

"They wanted me to sell, *sell mind you,* Wolf to them for a slave! That was after they asked if I was a slave!"

Gabe chuckled, "So, apparently you didn't sell him, so what did you say?"

Ezra just shook his head, "Not much, but when I cocked the hammer on my pistol, they got the message!"

Gabe laughed as he loosed the tether on Ebony and stepped aboard the big black, "I remember reading an article where the French admiral, Louis Antoine de Bougainville, who fought in the Seven Years War and against the British in our Revolutionary war, said that the 'Pawnee plays the same role in America that the Negroes do in Europe.' Of course, he was thinking more of Canada."

Ezra shook his head, "What is it with white people? Do they have to make slaves of everybody?" He spat the words as distasteful, something that came out only when talking about the dreadful subject of slavery.

"Uh, most of the Pawnee were taken and sold by other Indians, not whites. There is documentation of a time about a hundred years ago that a band of Apache brought quite a few captive Pawnee and others to a trading fair with the Spaniards in Santa Fe but there weren't enough buyers, so they beheaded them all right then and there."

They had ridden away from the post and were following the

south bank of the Kaw River when Ezra asked, "Where we goin'?" It was his first look through eyes that were not red with rage and he was surprised at the unfamiliar terrain by the river.

"We're gonna cross the Kaw. The trader said there was a good crossing just past this wide bend, current's easy, bottom's good, and should be an easy crossing. We'll camp on the other side."

"Oh," was all the response from Ezra, feeling somewhat quelled.

5 / Village

The heavy cloud cover made the rising sun work to give a silvery outline to puff ball clouds that shaded the land before them. The dimmed sunlight added a touch of cool to the air and the horses stepped lively as they held to the trail just inside the tree line. To their right was the wide river bottom of the Big Muddy meandering its way toward its distant confluence with the Mississippi. With wide sandy shoals, sandbars with deceiving quicksand, and deep-water currents hidden under the lightly rippling topwater, the river was to be avoided, although used as a guide to the northwest.

From the start of their journey, the three men worked to educate one another on the unique ways and language of the different people. Night Wolf had little exposure to the people outside of his tribe, with the only exception being times spent with French and Spaniard traders and the occasional visit from the black robes of the French missionaries. With sign language as the medium, they began learning the spoken languages of each other, as well as about the similarities and differences in cultures.

The first four days had proven interesting and challenging for the trio, each struggling with learning and sharing, but the constant discourse, a combination of sign language, Pawnee, English and French, kept all three involved. Occasionally lapsing into extended discussions, those sidebars usually started with a stroke of curiosity. "Wolf, we've been on the trail for four days now and you say we still have a couple days 'fore we get to your village, so, why is it that your bunch traveled so far to take one captive girl?"

"It is according to the vision of our shaman. He was shown that the young woman must be from the Missouria," answered Night Wolf.

"But the first bunch that attacked the Osage, why them if the vision was for a Missouria?" inquired Ezra.

"Our war leader, led us to the Osage. The Shaman did not say then if must be Missouria, for the Missouria, Otoe, and Osage are allies."

"But to travel such a distance for one captive, seems like a lot of trouble," surmised Gabe.

"To fulfill the ceremony of the Morning Star, all must be exact. Even the scaffold must be made the right way from the right wood and more," explained Wolf.

The men were contemplative for a short while until Gabe asked, "Your camp is on the south side of the Platte, that right?"

"Yes, for the *Tuhitsppiat (Village Stretching Out in the*

bottomlands) village of the *Tskirirara, (Skidi federation of the Pawnee)* that is our place. Now many will be gone from there on the buffalo hunt in the time of greening."

"But with loosing so many of your warriors, would the others still go on the hunt?" asked Gabe.

"Among our people, there are warriors that fight and then others who are the hunters. In a time of war with other people or an attack, then all, hunters and warriors will fight. The hunters would go on the early hunt even though the warriors had not returned."

"Will there still be people at the village?"

"Yes, the families of the warriors, although some will go on the hunt to help the other women with the butchering, but most would wait for their men to return. The old people will still be there. Our women have planted the crops already and will return to tend to them after the hunt," he added.

The morning of the fifth day started with a complete cloud cover that made the heavens look as if a vast downy blanket had been stretched across all of creation. The foggy fringe lay among the treetops as if caught on the branches and obscured the tips and muted the usual sounds of the woods. Squirrels stayed in their nests, owls slept on the branches, and birds of prey were grounded. The only sounds of the wild were the croaks of frogs from the river's edge. The fine morning mist dampened the blankets and the wet edge rubbed against Gabe's face, bringing him rudely awake. Before rising, he looked all around, making certain nothing was amiss, then rising, he tossed his blankets aside and started the morning fire.

"Well, if this isn't a dreary morning," mumbled Ezra as he crawled from his bedroll. He looked to Wolf's blankets to see them empty and with a glance to Gabe, he shrugged his shoulders, hands out as if to question the whereabouts of the Indian. Gabe pointed with his chin toward the thicker trees and Ezra understood, walking to the trees on the river's side of the clearing.

Mid-morning saw the foggy blanket burned off revealing a clear blue sky with a bright sun that warmed the riders' shoulders as they continued on their northward trail. The horses snatched mouthfuls of grass as they ambled prompting the riders to look for a nooning site. Wolf led the way and stretched out ahead of the two men trailing the pack horses, but they were surprised to ride up on him, down on one knee examining sign on the path.

Wolf stood, nodded toward the tracks, "Many riders, most white men, shod ponies, one hand and more."

"How many more," asked Gabe, "and what direction they headed?"

He held up one hand all fingers extended and the second hand with two, then three, fingers showing. He pointed to the northwest, "Same direction. Crossed here one, maybe two days before. One or two horses not ridden but carry heavy."

"So, could be packhorses," speculated Ezra.

Wolf nodded his head and swung back aboard the steel-dust. Gabe suggested, "Let's find us a place for our noonin' and give the horses a breather. I've got a feelin' we need to pick up the pace."

"Ummhumm, the hair on my neck's been standin' up all mornin'," shared Ezra.

"So, you think this bunch might be traders goin' to your village?" asked Gabe. They were on the last leg of their journey to Wolf's village and should reach the encampment before dusk.

"My people have often traded with the French and the Spaniards. These men have packhorses and could be traders," he stated, but his hesitancy in his answer told Gabe and Ezra that the man had reservations as to the intent of the men they followed.

By late afternoon, Wolf had slowed the pace and was extra vigilant and when asked by Gabe of his concern, he replied, "There should be lookouts watching for the village and there are none."

"You reckon all the men have gone on the hunt?" asked Gabe.

"No, there are always those that remain to protect the village. Young warriors, old men, and even some women are the lookouts and protectors."

They had gone less than another mile when Wolf turned from the trail and into the woods. Ezra and Gabe followed close behind as they came upon an abandoned campsite. Wolf dropped to the ground, followed by the two friends and all began to examine the sign around the camp. It soon became evident this had been the camp of the band thought to be traders, but Wolf said, "Two left with packhorses, and returned. Others also left and returned, but they came with others riding the same horses."

Gabe and Ezra looked to one another, both realizing that meant the men must have taken captives from the village. Ezra looked at Gabe and spat, "Slavers! Like them Frenchies we met at Choteau's!"

"Maybe, but don't go jumpin' the gun till we know for sure." He looked at Wolf, "Let's get a move on and go to your village."

The men stepped aboard the horses and reined around to take off at a canter. The two miles to Wolf's village were quickly covered by the ground eating pace and the men rode into a quiet and seemingly abandoned village. Wolf slid his horse to a stop and dropped to the ground. He looked around and called out in Pawnee, "Aho! I am Night Wolf of the *Tskirirara!* Where are my people?" He paced around nervously, looking from lodge to lodge. Finally, one blanket door was pushed aside as an old man stepped out and stood tall with his arms folded across his chest, waiting for Wolf to approach.

Wolf immediately walked up to the old man, stretched out his hand and greeted him with, "Aho, grandfather. I am Night Wolf. I was with the band of warriors that followed our war leader. I am all that survived."

The old man's surprise and dismay showed as his eyes revealed both alarm and sadness, but his expression remained stoic as he asked, "Who are these men?" pointing with his chin to Gabe and Ezra, now standing beside their mounts.

Wolf glanced back and looking at the elder of the village answered, "These are friends. They have tended my wounds and brought me to my people. What has happened here?"

"Men, such as these, came to trade while the hunters and others were gone on the hunt. But others came to the river where some women and children were tending to hides and more. They took some of our people."

Wolf was alarmed as he had yet to see his own family among those that had slowly come from their lodges. "How many were taken and who?"

"Four children, three girls and one boy, and three women. Your woman, Walking Bird, was one."

Wolf breathed deep, trying to control himself, but a mixture of anger and sorrow burned within him as he asked the old man, "Was there no one to stop them or go after them?"

"You and the others had gone south on the mission of the shaman. The hunters and others had gone on the hunt. All that remained were old people, women and children. We waited for you and the warriors to return. Your band should have been here."

"Aiiieee," screamed Wolf in anger and frustration, "I will go after them! I will bring them back!"

"What can you do against so many? You are but one!" asked the old man.

Wolf turned to look at Gabe and Ezra, turned away from

the old man and asked the two, "Did you hear what was said?"
"Uh, not all," answered Gabe and waited.

Wolf explained, then added, "I will go after these that
have taken my woman and the others."

Gabe looked at Ezra and asked, "You think we should go
with him?"

"Yeah! Anytime I can do somethin' 'bout slavin', you
know I'm gonna do it!" answered Ezra.

Gabe turned to look at Wolf, "If we leave now, we can get
a couple hours on the trail 'fore dark."

Wolf's eyes pinched and his forehead wrinkled as he
asked, "Why would you do this?"

"Remember what I said 'bout fightin' for my friends?" he
asked. When Wolf slowly nodded his head, still showing a
question on his face, Gabe continued, "Well, over the last
several days we kinda got used to you and I reckon you've
become a friend to us. So . . ." and shrugged his shoulders.
Then he asked, "You ready?"

Wolf slowly lifted his head to nod and turned toward the
elder, "We will go!" He looked back at Gabe, "I must get my
weapons from my lodge."

Within moments, instead of looking forward to a restful
night among new friends, the three men were on the trail,
taking the first few miles at a canter before letting the descending darkness drive them to camp. The horses were
spent as were the men and the thought of a hot meal, coffee,
and some rest beckoned.

6 / Chase

The trail of the band of slavers showed they were in no hurry. The horses kept to a steady walk, traveled in a single line, and stopped often. Men on horseback could easily make twenty to thirty miles in a day, provided there were no difficult obstacles to overcome. These were doing less than twenty and seldom left their camp for an early start. Their sign was easy to read by the experienced trackers and showed the women were not treated well. The children had all been bound hand and foot, released only when riding, and every horse rode double.

It was late on the second day out from the village that the trio came to the confluence of the Platte and the Missouri Rivers. "That tradin' post of James Mackay that Choteau told us about is just a couple miles upstream here. Accordin' to the sign we been following, I'm thinking those men stopped at the post for supplies, so we might get a little information from the man."

They were wary as they approached the post, a simple log structure that appeared to be little more than a log cabin. Nearby were several tipis of some Otoe, with the men giving hard looks at the Pawnee that rode with the white man. But the three paid little attention to the small village, noting no horses tethered at the post and no one, other than the Otoe, nearby. Gabe stepped down, handed the reins of Ebony to Ezra and walked through the open doorway.

Against one wall were stacks of boxes, barrels, and shelves loaded with goods. Stacks of pelts lined the back wall and against the side wall were a small table with two chairs, a single bunk with a man stretched out, forearm over his eyes, and snoring. Gabe stomped his feet to announce his presence and heard a groan from the man as he slowly sat up and glared at Gabe.

"Who're you an' whaddya want?" he grumbled.

"I'm Gabe and I want some information."

"Go away, I'm tired," mumbled the man and fell back on the bed.

Gabe walked to his side, looked down on him and said, "Answer my questions and you can go back to sleep, but I ain't leavin' till you answer!"

From his position on the bed, he looked up at the tall, broad-shouldered man with a no-nonsense scowl on his face, and James Mackay decided to abide by the man's request. He sat back up, rubbed his eyes, and stood beside the bed and said, "Alright. Whaddya wanna know?"

"Have you had anybody through here in the last day or so,

ridin' with several Indian women and kids?"

"Yeah, so?"

"Who were they and did they say anything about what they were doing or where they were going?"

"I don't know who they were, looked like Métis to me, they always have Injun women with 'em. Get them in ever now an' then. I've only been here 'bout a year now, so ain't seen a lot."

"How many men were there?"

"I dunno, half-dozen maybe. Only one of 'em came in to get their supplies. 'nother'n helped him carry it out an' load it."

"They say anything 'bout where they were goin'?"

"No, but I got the impression they were French, headin' back north. One man talked 'bout getting home, an' they spoke French to one another. Prob'ly didn't think I understood, but I do."

"These men stole those women and children from the Pawnee village. We ran into some of them down to Choteau's post and they tried to buy an Indian friend of ours. Talked about all the Indian slaves in Canada, so, I reckon you're right about them goin' north."

Gabe looked sternly at the man, shook his head, and turned away to leave. Without a look back, he mounted up and led the small group away. They knew they could pick up the trail easily enough, and knowing the slavers were heading back to Canada helped them in their plan to overtake the bunch and hopefully rescue the captives.

They wanted to shake the dust off their feet from the trader's place and put some miles behind them before they put in to camp. Once settled, they sat around the fire, considering the possibilities of their rescue attempt.

"I don't think just chargin' in shootin' will be the best. Near as we can tell there's at least six of 'em and we won't know where they will be in relation to the captives," started Gabe.

"As much as I'd like to just sit back and shoot 'em like targets on a fence, I do think you're right about that," agreed Ezra.

Both men looked at Wolf who sat on the trunk of a downed cottonwood, looking pensive and stoic. When he looked up, he was surprised the two men were looking at him and obviously awaiting a reply. He asked, "Why you look at me?"

"We want to know what you think would be the best way to approach the men that took your wife?"

He scowled, snatched his knife from the scabbard and snarled, "I will take them in their sleep and cut their throat," and as he spoke, he went through the motions of cutting a man's throat. "I will spit in their face and take their scalp, but I will burn it in the fire so it will not stink in my lodge!"

Ezra and Gabe looked at one another and nodded, each thinking he was glad he would not be on the receiving end of Wolf's vengeance. Gabe said, "You know, I think he might be right. 'Course, we'll have to make that call when we catch up to 'em. But if we can get to some in the dark and cut down the odds or even free the captives, that might be best."

"Well, first, let's get us some sleep and an early start tomorrow. Maybe we can catch up to 'em come dark, then decide," declared Ezra.

Gabe stood, stretched and spread out the coals of the fire, not needing the warmth in the night, but wanting coals for their morning fire. The men turned in, choosing to let the horses be their early warning in the event of any danger, for each of the men were light sleepers and felt no one could take them by surprise, not even in the dark. But as Gabe lay, hands clasped behind his head as he stared at the stars, he thought, *If we're confident no one can take us in the night, what makes us so different from the slavers?* It was with that thought ruminating in his mind that he finally drifted off to sleep.

They were on the trail before first light, Wolf scouting far ahead of the two friends that led the pack horses. Ezra had been unusually quiet, and Gabe asked, "What's got you so somber this morning?"

Ezra glanced at his friend, shook his head, "It's just the idea that anyone can take another and enslave them for the rest of their lives and no one do anything about it! Did I tell you 'bout the time when you were at the University and some slave catchers tried to take me as a runaway and put me in chains?"

Gabe scowled, unbelieving, for the two men shared most everything with one another, and for something as serious as this, he was surprised his friend had kept it to himself. "No, you've never said anything of the sort. When did this happen?"

"It was that open winter after Christmas, you remember, when we didn't get any snow until late January?"

"Yeah, that was my last year at University and I was loaded up with classes and didn't have any time to do anything but study. The one time when we had good weather in January, and I couldn't get outside for nothing!"

"Yeah, that's the one. I had been to my father's church to take him his lunch. You know how my mother was, thinking he always had to have a hot lunch. Anyway, I was on my way back and these two white men pulled up alongside and one of 'em jumped me, held me till the other'n jumped down and helped him. I had just about got free of the first man, until the second hit me over the head with somethin'. When I woke up, I was bound and gagged and in the back of the wagon. They were just pullin' away and I sat up, saw one of my father's parishioners and tried to holler, but I was gagged. I guess he saw my big eyes and knew somethin' was wrong. He hollered at the men, but they cursed him and took off.

"Anyway, Brother Clark, he's the one that saw me, went to my father and they got some men together and came after me. Those two men apparently didn't think they had any-thing to fear, cuz I heard 'em talkin' 'bout the reward they expected, and if they didn't get a suitable reward, they would just sell me. Since the only one that saw 'em was a colored man, they weren't concerned about getting caught. We was just at the edge of town when they pulled into Smitty's livery. They had an agreement with that old man to lock up any captured runaways in his tack room so they drug me from the wagon, and I tried to fight 'em, but couldn't. They put me in the tack room, threw me on the floor, didn't even take off the ropes and gag, and left. They was walkin' back to their hotel when Brother Clark recognized 'em. So, Pa and his two deacons, Brutus and Justis, you remember them, they're the ones Pa used to illustrate how big Goliath was, they blocked the walkway and those two white men thought they'd just push their way past, but those brothers wouldn't have it.

"Then Pa asked 'em, polite like, to take him to where they had the man they said was a runaway, said he wanted to pray for his parishioner, but they wouldn't. So, Brutus picked up one, tucked him under his arm, and Justis did the same with the other'n, and they carried 'em to the livery. Ol' Smitty saw 'em coming and was at the door, unlocking it when they came in. When Pa saw me all trussed up, he turned on those two slave catchers and read to them from the Scripture. Course what he had to say was from the first book of Reverend Blackwell and while he preached, the two deacons held them about a foot off the ground by their ears, just to make sure they heard correctly. They tried kicking and hitting and such, but when they resorted to cursing, Pa did something I'll never forget. He stuffed their mouths full of horse apples, just so they'd stay quiet and listen. You know how folks get restless when the sermon goes too long, well, Pa said he'd keep preaching until they quit kickin' and such.

So, they hung there real still, so, Pa nodded to the deacons to let 'em go, but not before he admonished them about how leaving Philadelphia would be best for their health."

Ezra shook his head and added, "So, ever since, that first-hand experience about being taken to be sold into slavery made me just a little gun shy. That's one of the reasons I came along with you on this 'grand adventure'!"

Gabe said, "I'm surprised you didn't tell me about that, why didn't you?"

"I was tryin' too hard to forget it!" he declared.

"Here's something that'll rub you wrong too. A few years back, the Spanish governor Alejandro O'Reilly, who was over this part of the country, he banned the taking of Natives as slaves, banned the whole business of the slavery of Indians. Seems he thought it was causing too much trouble, because the tribes were raiding each other and taking captives to sell into the slave trade. People kept doin' it anyway, so the new governor, Esteban Rodriguez Miro, republished that decree and allowed the Indians to sue for their freedom. That pretty much stopped it, at least here in this territory."

"So, there is a law against them taking Natives for slaves?" asked Ezra.

"That's right, but these men are taking them to Canada, and it's not against the law there. Now, here's the kicker, if they had taken coloreds, there is no law against that!"

Ezra reined up, turned to look at his friend, "You mean, if they had taken me, even though my mother is a Black Irish and not a true colored, that would have been lawful, but it's against the law to take Indians?"

"That's right," answered Gabe.

Ezra looked incredulous, wide eyed, furrowed brow, and cheek muscles flexing. His nostrils flared as he shook his head side to side, then he turned his eyes back to the trail, urged his mount forward and mumbled as he moved ahead. After a moment, he turned in his seat, glared at Gabe and said, "Guess I'll just have to show them the error of their ways, maybe even preach to them like my Pa did!"

Gabe grinned, and chuckled, then answered, "You do that, friend, and I'll take the collection!"

7 / Slavers

The French slavers had become accustomed to letting the women do the work in setting up their camp. Although the tending of the horses was done by the men, the gathering of firewood, building the cookfire, and preparing the meals was all done by the women. The Frenchmen proved to be a lazy lot, typical of those that had slaves to do all the menial labor for them, and they sat around watching the women work and talking about them and their plans in French, believing none of their captives understood.

Gaspard Dubois was the leader of the bunch of slavers, having turned from his work as a *voyageur* working for the Northwest Company. It was through that company and the Hudson's Bay company that he had recruited this band of misfits, all former trappers that preferred selling a captive Indian for upwards of two thousand franc to wading in the icy streams for a beaver pelt that was worth no more than fifteen franc. Dubois had already calculated their total for the captives to be over ten thousand francs, or two thousand dollars. He would take his share of five hundred dollars and each of the others would have three hundred, more than they could make in two years of trapping.

An angry Raphael Bernard approached Dubois carrying a saddle, threw it on the ground at Dubois' feet and snarled, "Someone's put a knife to the girth! If I hadn't seen that, I woulda been dumped at the first sudden move of the horse!"

"Who did it?" asked Dubois.

"I think it was that squaw that's been ridin' with me. She ain't been none too friendly and fights me at ever turn! She needs a lesson in how to treat a man!" snarled Bernard. He was the most disliked of the bunch, always complaining and griping, pushing his chores on the others, and vulgar in his manner. No one had ever known him to get any water past his wrists nor ankles and his beard drew flies like a week-old carcass. Everyone avoided him and the captive squaw that rode with him had become considerably more surly than the others. None of the men could blame her for her obvious revulsion.

"Right now that squaw's worth more to us than you are so watch your step! If anything happens to her, it'll come out of your share! Got that?" growled Dubois. He was half a head taller than Bernard and outweighed him by at least thirty pounds. The other men respected Dubois and feared him because his reputation had always been as a fighter and killer. When Bernard started to respond, he grunted and bent to pick up the saddle to begin the repairs. Two of the men had watched the interchange between their leader and the disgruntled Bernard and one, Louis Petit, asked Dubois, "We could easily do without him, and no one would miss him."

Dubois scowled at Petit, "We'll tend to that when the time comes. For right now, we're mighty close to that village of the Omaha and we don't need to get them upset. I was hoping to do some trading with them, see if they have any captives to sell."

Bernard had stretched out a piece of bison leather traded from the Otoe along the top edge of a greyed cottonwood. The cut on the latigo of the girth on the saddle was almost all the way through and the entire latigo would have to be replaced. With the bison skin stretched out, he lay the latigo atop it to use as a pattern and with his skinning knife he began the long straight cut. He looked up to see the Pawnee squaw named Grey Dove watching him cut the leather. She stood with fists on her hips, glaring at the dirty slaver, hatred showing in her eyes that were slightly squinted, her lip snarled at the corner, and her nostrils flared. She said in Pawnee, which Bertrand couldn't understand other than the inflection and expression, "Your stink fouls the air! You smell as if you're dead already!"

He stood and snarled at the woman, "I don't know what you said, but I know you're the one that cut this! I should cut you for this!"

Dove did not understand the Frenchman but caught his meaning when he flashed the knife towards her. She cleared her throat and brought up a gob of snot and spat at him. She spun around to leave, but the foul man lunged and grabbed her long braid and jerked her back to him. He growled, "Spit at me, will ya!" and brought his knife across her throat. Her eyes flared, and she tried to spit again, but only blood came as life seeped out of her eyes.

He held her against his chest, plunged the knife into her chest, jerked it out and drove it through her ribs again and again. He knew she was dead, but he kept stabbing her for his own pleasure. His back was to the men at the fire, and he held her body against him, then slowly lowered it to the ground, growling as he let her drop to her side in a clump. He wiped his knife on his britches leg and turned back to his work on the leather. She lay alongside the big cottonwood log that he used for his hide carving and wasn't visible to the others, the lowering darkness and long shadows of the trees masking her form.

Walking Bird and Blue Flower looked to the men, motioning that the food was ready and Gaspard led the others to dish up their venison stew and pour their cups full of rum. Louis Petit called Bernard, "Hey Raphael, food's ready!"

"Yeah, yeah, I'm coming," he growled, slipping his knife back in the scabbard and starting for the fire.

Walking Bird frowned, looking for Grey Dove, having noticed her walking toward the trees beyond the log where Bernard had been working. While the men dished up their food, she started toward the log and softly called her name. With no answer, she looked to the woods and called her name a little louder. She walked past the log, searching the tree line, and called again. When no answer came, she turned back to the fire and saw the crumpled form in the dark shadow beside the log. Three quick steps brought her to the side of the still form, and she knelt down beside her friend, pushed at her arm thinking to awaken her. But when the body rolled to its back, Walking Bird gasped, her hand to her mouth, and she stood. She pointed to Bernard and shouted, "You killed her! You! You killed her!" and stomped toward him, anger flaring in her eyes, her arms stiff at her sides, and she screamed, "You should die!!"

The other men were spellbound as they watched the angry woman, and even though they didn't clearly understand her words, they knew what she meant. Gaspard stepped in front of her, pushed her back and turned on Bernard, asking him in French, "What did you do?" Before the man could answer he turned and commanded Louis Petit, "Go, look!" nodding toward the log. Bird was fuming and through gritted teeth and snarling lips, she growled in French, *"Il l'a tuée!"*

Dubois glowered at Bernard, "Did you kill that squaw?"

"She had it coming! She cut the girth and then she spit in my face!" he growled, spitting to the side to show his own disgust.

Without a word of warning, Dubois smashed his plate full of stew in the man's face and brought up a meaty fist into his gut, bending him over, then hit him on the side of the head with such force the Bernard stumbled backwards across the fire, screaming and cursing. He started to get up, but Dubois had come to his side and stood over him, put his big foot square on the man's chest and threatened, "That squaw's worth comes out of your share! And if you so much as look like you're going to touch another one of those Indians, I will personally cut your throat and spit in your face while you bleed to death!"

"Now, get yourself up and down to the creek. It'd do you good and us too, if you'd jump in and clean up. You stink!" barked Dubois, turning back to the pot by the fire to refill his plate.

Bernard grunted and grumbled, wiped most of the food from his face and trudged away toward the creek. As he left, Petit asked Dubois, "You think he'll wash?"

"Non, he'll put his face in the water, wipe it off and think he's clean," answered the big man, starting on his stew. "We'll cross the Missouri River tomorrow, then maybe we can push him in and make him swim to shore." The two men laughed, and as Louis Petit repeated what their leader said, the other men laughed together. They were all hopeful of anything being done about the smelly Bernard.

Gaspard Dubois had commandeered Walking Bird and kept her at his side when they turned in for the night. Louis Petit had taken Blue Flower, and the other men had each taken one of the girls. But this night, Raphael Bernard would have no one to warm his blankets. The lone boy, Badger, was tied to a tree and a blanket thrown over him. Although the men had been cautioned to not mistreat any of the captives, he was striving to keep the females unharmed and to retain their value. They were treated as trade goods and the value was dependent on their condition, so his concern was solely a monetary not moral one.

8 / Confrontation

It was evident by the tracks the slavers and their captives made no effort to cover their sign, showing Gabe that the Frenchmen believed no one was following. Each day the trio pushed themselves to cover more ground and gain on the group, and each day the sign was fresher as they drew closer. With the terrain a monotonous flat land with short stretches of rolling timber covered hills, there was little opportunity for the pursuers catch sight of the kidnappers.

At the approach of dusk on the fourth day north of the confluence of the Platte and Missouri Rivers, the trail of the slavers had stayed inland from the river and took to the high ground above the boggy bottomland. The Big Muddy often changed its course, leaving rich bottomland or wide swamp lands that held quicksand, willows and cattails, but no solid ground to travel. Wolf had drawn up, stood in his stirrups and shielded his eyes to search the area beyond their slight promontory. When Gabe and Ezra came alongside,

he pointed, "They make camp soon, maybe now in trees."
He pointed away from the river, "Big village of the Omaha,
there. Many lodges."

Gabe reached back and brought out his brass telescope,
stretched it out toward the village and frowned. He looked
at Wolf, "How big is that village?" and lifted the scope to his
eye again. In the distance, the treetops showed a low-lying
wispy cloud of smoke, unmistakable as the smoke from many
cookfires. But the terrain and trees prevented any view of the
village itself.

"The *U-Mo'n-Ho'n* people call it *Ton-wa-tonga* or Big
Village. Their chief is Blackbird. There are as many lodges in
that village as days in two moons."

Gabe lowered the scope to look at Wolf, thinking, "That's
sixty lodges!" He frowned as he thought of a village that size
then asked, "How many people in each lodge?"

Wolf thought a moment, then flashed both hands with all
fingers raised, three times.

Gabe stared at the man, then looked to Ezra, "That would
be over a thousand people. That's bigger'n most towns of the
white men!" He looked back at Wolf, "Are they friendly?"

"They trade with the French and the Spanish as well as
other tribes. They are friendly, yes," answered Wolf.

As they spoke, Gabe continued to scan the hills and trees
in the general direction indicated by Wolf where the slavers
might make camp. They were on a bald flat-topped mesa that
stood about three hundred fifty feet above the river bottom
and offered a good panorama of the surrounding country.

Suddenly he stopped, leaned slightly forward and adjusted the scope. His breath came in shallow draws, as he moved the scope slightly side to side. "There!" He whispered. He lowered the scope, handed it to Ezra, "There's a thin trail of smoke through that dip in the hills, very faint. I think the women are intentionally showing smoke."

Ezra searched in the direction indicated, then paused, "Ummhumm. Tain't much, but I think you're right." He handed the scope to Wolf who accepted it but had never seen nor used a telescope before and Gabe, seeing the man's frustration, showed him what to do and handed the scope back. When he looked, he pulled it down, looked at it and then to Gabe who nodded, grinning, and motioned for him to look again. Wolf slowly raised the scope to his eye and held the brass tube steady and uttered a groan as he took in the sight. When he lowered the scope, he looked in the same location, then down at the scope as he handed it to Gabe, slowly shaking his head, eyes wide and eyebrows raised.

"That's not more'n an hour away, so we can make it closer and hold up 'fore we sneak in and see what they've got," suggested Gabe. He looked to the others and with no response, he motioned for Wolf to move out, his mind already working on a possible plan for the rescue of the captives. From what he was able to see before they moved off the mesa, the band of slavers was camped at the edge of the trees near the bottomland of the Missouri. He knew they would have to have a better look-see before they decided what to do, but he also knew they would have to use the cover of darkness for their attack. Being outnumbered two to one and with captives probably used as shields, they couldn't risk an all-out attack with gunfire endangering the women and children.

They stayed in the thicker timber, picking their own trail, no longer following the tracks of the band of slavers. The big river held close to the timber where they were, forcing them higher up the hillside, but its course pushed into the flats, following a previous bed away from the boggy bottom land near the timber. Wolf led them to higher ground that overlooked the barren sandy flats that showed as pale colors in the waning light of day. When their chosen route took them to the top of a timbered knoll, Gabe surmised they were atop the big hill above the camp of the slavers. Using only signs, Wolf indicated Gabe's guess was correct and the three men stepped down from their mounts, standing quietly once together.

As they looked around and through the timber, Gabe tried to get in the minds of the Frenchmen. They had shown themselves to be savvy in the wilderness, but also lazy with their ways. He whispered to the others, pointing to a wide valley to their left that cut its way between the hills, "I think there's a stream in the bottom there, and when we left their trail, they were headed in that direction. If they were to expect anyone to follow, they'd look for them to come along behind them on their trail through that valley." He paused, looking to the right towards the river, "I think we'd do better comin' at 'em from down thataway," pointing to the tree line that shadowed the flats beside the river.

The flats stretched about a mile and a half to the river, "If we stay inside the tree line, we'll have good cover all the way to their camp. We can leave the horses down there," nodding below them at the edge of the trees. "But," he lifted his eyes to the lowering darkness and to the half moon that seemed to hang amidst a handful of flickering stars that struggled to light their lanterns, "we'll give 'em time to get sound asleep 'fore we go near. I figger to sneak up on 'em to get the lay of their camp, then we'll make a plan to strike 'em 'fore daylight."

They moved back in the deep timber, picked their way through the dark shadowy woods and followed the contour of the hill to the edge of the flats. Gabe guessed them to be about two miles from the slaver's camp, and five miles from the Omaha village. It would be a cold camp, no fire to give away their location, and they would try to get a little rest before moving out for their attack. The time was not spent in their blankets. Each man busied himself readying his weapons, sharpening the knives, reloading the pistols and rifles, and more, all the while thinking about the coming fight. With no fire, they allowed their night vision to develop as they worked at their tasks. Gabe spoke softly, "I've been thinking. Maybe we should make this a quiet fight, I'm not too sure about that Omaha village over yonder. I wouldn't want to get them all riled up and come after us, since we're in their country and all. What do you think, Wolf? Wouldn't your people get a little upset if some white men came in and started a fight, even if it wasn't against them?"

"Yes. Any fight near our village would cause us to believe it was an attack against us and we would fight!" he answered.

"I know you said the Omaha were friendly enough, but . . ." he said, shaking his head.

"But you fight with your rifles and pistols, they are not silent," stated Wolf.

Gabe grinned, "Oh, we have other weapons. Show him, Ezra."

Ezra chuckled, stood and went to his gear stacked near the trees beside the horses, retrieved his war club and returned. Often described as a gunstock warclub because of its silhouette shape that resembled that of a rifle stock, the ironwood club with the inlaid stones and beads with its halberd blade made Wolf lean back as Ezra swung it in a swooping arch. He handed it to Wolf to heft and the man stood, holding the fiendish weapon, then swung it back and forth, grinning as he looked at Ezra. When he handed it back, he looked to Gabe to see the white man stringing an unusual bow that once strung bent back on itself.

Wolf scowled and walked closer to see this weapon in the hands of his friend. Gabe extended the bow toward Wolf who accepted it and held it carefully, examining the feel and shape of the unusual weapon. When strung, the Mongol bow is about the same length as the traditional bow of the Natives, but the recurve of the shape gives it more power. After giving it a once-over, Wolf lifted it and placed his fingers on the twisted horsehide string and started to pull. But he was surprised when the string stayed taut and he didn't move it but an inch or so with great effort. He looked at Gabe, then at the bow and pulled again, but was again unsuccessful. He asked, "It is so tight, you cannot use such a weapon."

Gabe accepted it as Wolf extended it toward his friend and Gabe reassured him, "Oh, I can use it quite well. It takes a lot of practice and effort, but this bow is much more effective than you think."

"Which brings to mind, I know the two of you are wanting some personal vengeance on this bunch and I won't try to deny you that right. So, once we get a good look at their layout, one or both of you can go in amongst 'em and do your deed. I'll watch over things with my bow, but I'll also have my pistols at hand, just in case," explained Gabe. He lifted his eyes to the night sky, "So, if we're ready, let's take a walk. We should get there at about the right time."

Gabe yielded the lead to Wolf. Although the three men were equally capable and adept in the woods and at stealthily moving through the woods, Gabe knew Wolf was more invested with his wife being one of the captives. The three were like shadows in the darkness, the moonlight showing the way and bouncing off their shoulders. Their movement was the only sign of their presence. It was the scent of smoke that dropped Wolf to one knee, hand held high to stay the others. Gabe and Ezra's flared nostrils caught the same smell, and they froze in place, searching the dim light for the camp. For those unaccustomed to the night, they often think that nothing can be seen in the darkness. But there is more light from the moon and stars than most believe, and the men used every bit of light in their search.

They searched for shapes rather than detail. Listened for the sounds uncommon to the woods. Watched for the slightest movement. "There!" whispered Wolf, pointing to the edge of trees where horses were tethered. One stomped, another snorted, one shifted his weight in the slightest of movements, but all three men had noted the picket line that held the horses. Their eyes moved to the dim glow of ash covered coals, and slowly began to identify the sleeping forms. After mentally mapping the camp, Gabe motioned for them to move back into the trees.

"With only one tied to that tree, it looks like each of the men has a captive with him in his blankets. That the way you see it?" whispered Gabe, looking from one man to the other.

"Yeah, an' it's hard to tell which is which, unless we get more light," observed Ezra.

"When we are closer, we can tell. The men are all bigger!" growled Wolf, his hand on his knife handle, gripping and releasing as he thought about his woman in the blankets with another man.

"Here's the way I'm thinkin'. Wolf, you circle around and come from the upper end. Ezra, you follow him till you come 'bout even with the tree where that boy is tied. I'll be at the edge of the trees on the low side, that'll keep any of 'em from gettin' away. We'll give the cry of the nighthawk, just one, to show you're ready. When I give the deeper boom of their call, that's your signal to do your thing."

Both Ezra and Wolf nodded, then Gabe added, "Wolf,

I know you're goin' after your woman first, and Ezra, you free the boy and if you're of a mind, sneak into their camp and bid them good-night in your own way. I'll stand ready with my bow, just in case some of 'em get restless." The men parted, moving into the deep shadows as silently as a owl in the night, on the hunt, circling its prey, waiting to attack.

9 / Reprisal

The early morning dew lay heavy on the matted leaf floor of the woods. Gabe felt the moisture through his moccasins knowing the dampness would further silence their approach. When he was within about twenty yards of the camp, he dropped to hands and knees, his bow across his back and tunic over his pistols to keep the dampness away. He moved about five yards closer, then dropped to his belly to watch the camp. Nothing moved, but the snores, grunts and groans from the sleeping men blended with the occasional stomping hoof of the horses, gave ample indication of the location of each of the sleepers. As he watched, he saw one large figure, blanket across his legs, showing he was alone. All the others had a captive close beside them, most with a leg or an arm across their body.

One form jerked, tried to sit up, but was yanked back down to her back. In that instant, Gabe saw a short tether attached to the wrist of the captive. He waited, watching the pair that had moved, but soon they lay silent, even breathing coming from the man as he snored with every breath. Gabe slid closer, moving slower than a turtle, showing no visible movement that would give him away. His goal was a sizable bur oak tree that was slightly isolated from the rest, but with a tall straight and broad trunk that would give him perfect cover.

He used the tree as a shield and slowly rose to stand. The black night was slowly greying with the thin line in the eastern sky heralding the arrival of another day. He checked his pistols, unconcerned with the two French double barreled with their unusual waterproof pans, but he checked the Bailes turnover carefully. Satisfied, he brought the bow from his back, drew three arrows from the quiver than hung at his side, stabbed two slightly into the ground at his feet then nocked the third. He slowly moved to the side of the tree, staying close so his silhouette would not distinguish his form from the rough barked tree, and waited.

Then came the first tweet of the nighthawk which Gabe recognized as Ezra by the location of the call. Within moments, almost as an echo, came another shrill tweet. Both men were ready, and Gabe gathered a deep breath and let the booming sound of the nighthawk fill the darkness. The three men watched every form in the camp, being certain the calls of the nighthawk had not awakened the Frenchmen, and when satisfied, Ezra and Wolf showed themselves as nothing more than shadows in the darkness as they moved closer.

Ezra dropped to one knee beside the still form of the boy,

quickly placing a hand over his mouth, then cutting his bonds with the razor-sharp knife, the matching double of the Flemish knives carried by Gabe. When the boy was free, Ezra used hand signs to tell him to quietly move into the trees. A slow nod from the wide-eyed boy and Ezra moved back, watching the young man disappear silently into the woods. He knew the curious boy would be just out of sight but close enough to watch whatever was about to happen. He wouldn't abandon the women and girls.

Wolf moved on hands and toes resembling the movement of a large spider, knife held in his teeth, and came quickly to the side of a blanket covered mound. The two forms were lying on their side, the woman in front of the big man, his arm over her side and holding her close. His snoring blew wisps of the woman's hair and she moved slightly with each snort, showing Wolf she was not sound asleep. He moved behind the man, sank to one knee, then suddenly placed his hand over the man's mouth at the same time driving the blade of his knife into his back, parting the ribs and driving into his heart. The man jerked, but Wolf moved the blade of the knife side to side, ripping through the man's innards. Wolf's knee on the man's side, his hand at his mouth, and the knife driven deep kept the man from any additional movement. Wolf waited, jerked out the knife, pushed the man to his back and slit his throat ear to ear. The woman had jerked away but instantly recognized her man and though tethered at her wrist, she pulled away to give Wolf the space needed.

Gaspard Dubois' eyes stared into the dark heavens, the

only glimpse of a heavenly home he would ever have, and Wolf spat in his face. He turned to look at his woman, saw the tether and quickly cut through the leather bond. He turned back to Dubois and ran his knife along the hairline of his forehead and around the dome, grabbed a handful of hair and jerked off the scalp. He handed the scalp to his woman and with a head nod, sent her into the trees.

Wolf looked at the nearest blanket, saw the man start to move, and dropped to a low crouch, unmoving. The man, Louis Petit, had been lying with Blue Flower in the same way as Dubois, both on their sides, facing the same way, the woman drawn close. But he rolled over, jerked at the tether, growled and started to sit up. He saw Wolf and started to speak, but the whisper of an arrow came, and the shaft sunk into the man's chest, pushing him to the ground. He kicked and tried to cry out but was choked on his own blood. Blue Flower sat up, looked wide eyed to Wolf and held up her wrist and tether. Wolf quickly cut through the rawhide and motioned for her to go to the trees.

Ezra had moved from the tree where the boy was tied, saw Wolf moving toward a sleeping figure and picked one of his own nearby. He crawled toward the head of the man whose snoring would have masked the sound of an approaching horse. Once within reach, Ezra rose to one knee, put his hand over the man's mouth and slit his throat in one quick motion. The man's eyes flared, he kicked off the blanket and tried to move, but the blood came in gushing spurts and quickly drained the life from the slaver. Ezra wiped his knife on the blanket, cut the tether of the frightened girl, now sitting up and staring at this black ghost of the night, and pointed to the woods and motioned for silence. The girl quickly scrambled to her feet and ran to the trees, never looking back.

"Hey!" came a shout from a man that was sitting up and looking toward Wolf, he was grabbing for his rifle when the arrow took him in the throat. He grabbed at the shaft with both hands but fell back with wide eyes staring at the grey line of morning, the last day he would ever see. His shout had caused the others to stir and blankets were kicked aside as the two, Raphael Bernard and another, scrambled for weapons. The foul Frenchman Bernard laid his hand on his rifle, but the moccasined foot of Wolf stopped him. He looked up to see the bloody knife of the Indian move to his throat, and the Indian grab his hair. Bernard froze in place, eyes wide, mouth open and stuttering as Wolf pulled him to his feet. Wolf stepped behind him, still holding his hair, but with the knife at his throat.

The one remaining man, Etienne Barbou, was the youngest of the group, probably no more than twenty, but just as dirty and just as guilty as the others. He had grabbed his rifle, but before he could bring it to his shoulder, he saw Gabe step from behind the tree, an arrow fully drawn and pointed at him. He let go his weapon and held one hand high, the other still tethered to a girl at his side. His mouth was open and his eyes flaring as he felt his heart beating as if it wanted out of his chest. He started to rise but wet himself and looked to the girl who scooted as far away from him as the tether would allow. Ezra stepped to the side of the girl, cut her tether, and motioned her to the trees.

The women had been watching and now came from the trees, the boy and girls with them. Walking Bird went to the side of her man and looked to Gabe and Ezra, then to her man and asked in Pawnee, "Who are these that fight with you?"

Wolf chuckled, "They are friends." He nodded toward Gabe and said, "That is Gabe," then toward Ezra, "He is Ezra."

Gabe came near, still holding his bow with an arrow nocked, but letting off on the draw and lowering it before him. He looked to Walking Bird, "Where is the other woman?"

She glared at Bernard, spat on him, and said, "He killed her." Bernard had stepped back when she spat and tried to lunge forward but the knife at his throat stopped him.

Gabe asked, "Were you or the others mistreated?"

Walking Bird dropped her eyes, glanced toward Blue Flower, and both looked at Gabe. Neither woman answered, but their countenance with tight jaws, squinted eyes, flaring nostrils told him all he needed to know. Although they were speaking in stilted Pawnee and French, the expressions of the women told more than their words. Gabe looked to Wolf, "You think we should let the women decide what to do with these two?" He knew that the women of the natives often participated in the torture and deaths of captives, usually showing a greater tendency for the horrific than the men.

"It is custom of my people that the one wronged has the right to repay," answered Wolf.

"Well, it looks like you don't need our help. We'll just mosey on back to get our gear and horses, then we'll come along and help you with the rest," answered Gabe, nodding to Ezra for him to come along as well. The two friends, turned away, and started into the rising sun to make their way back to their camp. Little was said as they walked the two plus miles back to where the horses waited, but as they came to their makeshift camp, Ezra asked, "What do you suppose they'll do?"

"Dunno, but I've heard some pretty gruesome stories about what some of those Native women can do. Those women and kids have been put through a lot and I just didn't trust myself with those two." He shook his head, "When I thought about what might have happened, all I could do is to think of how the same thing could be done to those men. After all, doesn't the Bible say somewhere *'an eye for an eye'*?"

Ezra shook his head, chuckled, "Yeah, it does. But on those same pages it says to turn the other cheek and go the extra mile. Now, what we did to rescue those captives, that's one thing, but to deliberately torture and kill someone, that's somethin' else."

"Well, it's not like we could haul 'em off to some sheriff somewhere and thrown 'em in jail!" declared Gabe. "If those men had come upon us unexpected, they would have shown no mercy and wouldn't have given another thought to killing us," argued Gabe, bending to pick up his saddle. He stepped beside Ebony, put the blanket on the horse, smoothed it out and swung the saddle aboard. He reached under the big black's belly and grabbed the girth and threaded the latigo and drew it tight, jammed his knee into the stubborn horse's ribs for him to let out his breath and pulled the latigo tight and tied it off. He turned to look at Ezra, "So, what else could we have done?"

"I reckon I coulda read to 'em from the Scriptures like my Pa done, but I didn't have two monster deacons in my 'Amen' corner to make sure he understood. Then again, I don't think it'd do evil-doers like them much good," answered Ezra, saddling his bay. The packhorses were rigged and once Gabe unstrung his bow and put it in the case, hung the quiver of arrows on the cantle, and put the saddle pistols in their holsters beside the pommel, and Ezra had done likewise, they mounted up and started back to the waiting Wolf and now freed captives.

As they approached the camp, Gabe and Ezra both sensed something was wrong. It was too quiet, there was no talking, no movement, nothing. A quick glance told the men the horses had been cut loose and although several grazed nearby, some were gone. When they rounded the trees at the edge of the clearing, they saw the small cluster of girls, holding on to one another, the boy standing nearby. Next to the oak Gabe had used for cover, the woman, Blue Flower, was on her knees, rocking back and forth, sobbing. Before her lay the bodies of Wolf and Walking Bird.

10 / Retaliation

Gabe could tell at a glance that both Wolf and Walking Bird were dead, and his rage boiled within him. He had been wrong to leave the big smelly Frenchman alone with Wolf and the women, but he had only thought of their need for vengeance rather than the danger, believing Wolf to be more than a match for the slavers. Now, with the burden of self-imposed blame, he jerked the head of Ebony around, snarled at Ezra, "You stay with this woman and those kids! I'm goin' after that murderin' scum!"

Without waiting for a reply, he dropped the lead of the pack horse and put heels to the black's ribs. The big stallion lunged ahead, eager to take up the chase and within two leaps was at a full gallop tearing across the grassy flats toward the Big Muddy. The tracks of the fleeing men were less than an hour old and the running horse had dug deep in the soft soil. Gabe reined up at the river's edge, pulled the Ferguson from the scabbard, lay it across the seat behind the pommel, stuffed his belt pistol in the pommel, and lay the oiled case of the Mongol bow atop the rifle. He kicked his feet free of the stirrups and kneed the black into the water. With almost two hundred yards of current to fight, he knew his Ebony was up to it, and as soon as the horse buoyed in the deep water, he slid from the saddle to the downstream side, and let the stallion have his way, holding to the tie straps by the pommel.

His neck stretched out and his long legs moving, Ebony made steady headway against the current. Gabe shivered in the cold water, his teeth chattering, but he floated alongside, kicking his feet to give what little help he could, and within moments, he felt the big black gain footing in the soft river bottom. The current pushed against them, but the stallion found solid ground and soon rose from the water. Once atop the bank, Gabe grabbed the Ferguson and bow case and stood aside as the black rolled his skin and shook off the excess water. With a couple more steps on dry ground, Ebony craned his neck around to look at Gabe, waiting for him to mount.

Gabe hung the bow case under the left fender leather, held the Ferguson tight and swung aboard. He would wait for the scabbard to dry more before entrusting his rifle to the damp leather. A quick glance caught sight of the tracks of the fleeing horse and he kicked his stallion to the trail. He was confident in his mount, knowing he had the strength and stamina as well as speed to soon overtake the slaver, and he let him have his head. Within a few strides, the black stretched out, catching the wind in his mane and his tail flying behind him like a pirate's flag on a schooner. Gabe leaned over his pommel, stretching out on Ebony's neck, catching the flying mane in his face, and reaching down to pat his neck and encourage the animal in his run.

The Big Muddy flowed wherever it wanted and often altered its course by the amount of run-off water in the spring and had apparently done just that this year. After a short stretch of brush and timber, they came to the old riverbed and the tracks of the slaver led directly into the uncertain bottom land. The sun-dried mud had cracked and curled, making the old riverbed look like a frying pan full of a new bride's attempt at biscuits. The big black crashed through the dried crust and the mud and bog beneath pulled at his hooves, but he fought his way across to solid ground. The tracks of Bernard's horse showed it was no longer running and Gabe guessed the big man had assumed no one was following and chose to spare the animal. It was not unusual for even the most coarse behaving man to show care to his horse, knowing the animal could make the difference between life and death in the wilderness. Gabe also pulled Ebony back to a canter, still determined to catch the fleeing slaver without any more delay yet sparing his horse as well.

It was nearing mid-day when the horizon showed thicker timber. They had been traveling through the flats, buffalo grass turning green, early flowers adding color, bluestem and gramma showing a touch more color. He couldn't help thinking of the difference in this land and his home in Pennsylvania, he had grown to love the openness of the prairie and the freedom it offered. His mind was soon brought back to his mission as he turned aside from the tracks of the flee-ing slaver, believing the man might have taken cover in the trees.

He caught a glimpse of a thin line of smoke and thought it to be from a nooning cookfire of the slaver. He was about a half-mile from the tree line and he pointed the black away from the trail toward the thicker trees further away from the site of the smoke. There was nothing to indicate he had been seen so he pushed into the trees and saw a small river that wound its way to the southwest. That explained the stop and nooning of the slaver, the trees being the usual greenery that bordered the river.

He stepped down, tethered the black and stuffed one of the saddle pistols in his belt beside his belt pistol. With Ferguson in hand, he checked the loads, and started through the trees toward where he'd seen the thin line of smoke. His anger was driving him on, but he had to bring it in check, he couldn't allow anything to hinder his quest for vengeance.

Carefully working his way through the dense trees and brush, he watched every step although his stealth was aided by the fresh greenery that pushed through the matted leaves from the winter. Moving slowly, always in a bit of a crouch, and searching through the foliage for any scent of smoke or movement, he was brought to a sudden stop by the sound of a gruff voice. He recognized the snarl and snap of the filthy Frenchman but heard nothing else. He moved a little closer, keeping himself behind cover, but needing to see who the man was talking with, perhaps another trapper.

He was surprised to see the frail form of an Indian girl, sitting near the small fire, head hanging and staring at the dirt before her. Gabe thought, *I shoulda known he'd take one with him!* He stepped behind the nearest tree but the sudden scream from the girl brought him to the side, raising the Ferguson to fire. But the man was bent over the girl, she was sobbing, and he was muttering some curses in French, slapping the girl repeatedly.

Two long bounds brought Gabe to the side of the big man, he swung the butt end of the Ferguson up and smashed it into the side of the man's head, splattering his ear across the side of his face. The Frenchman momentarily slumped to the side, his hand at his ear and he stood and glared at the smaller Gabe and with a roar, raised his clasped hands overhead to strike down at Gabe. But the rangy blonde with the broad shoulders and angry snarl, ducked under the blow, driving the muzzle of the Ferguson into the bigger man's gut.

Bernard doubled over, both hands at his stomach as he gasped for air, stumbling to the side. He sucked deep and stood, eyes squinting, "I was hopin' you'd foller me!" he growled. "Now I'm gonna tear you apart 'fore I gut you like I did yore Injuns!" Gabe was surprised to hear the man speak in English, and guessed his background was more varied than expected. Bernard spread his arms wide and roared like the demons of hell as he charged the startled Gabe. But Gabe surprised the beast by tossing his rifle and pistols aside and dropping into a crouch, arms wide. Bernard expected to bear hug the smaller man like he had done so many while a pirate on the keelboats of the Mississippi. When he saw Gabe toss aside his weapons, he grinned and shook his head as he charged. He stretched out his arms to grab at the younger man, but Gabe stepped aside, grabbed Bernard's arm and gave him a hip roll, smashing the big man into the dirt and knocking the breath from him.

The Frenchman showed himself to be more agile than most men his size and he rolled over and sprang to his feet. He turned to look at his prey, and snarled again as he laughed and charged. Then the lithe blonde man in buckskins surprised the monster again by what he thought was a hop in the air, but he came down with both feet against the massive leg and knee, buckling the post of the beast and dropping him to the ground. Gabe rolled over, jumped to his feet and sidestepped around the man, taunting him, "C'mon big boy, I thought you were gonna tear me limb from limb, what's the matter?"

Now the more wary adversary held his fists before him, staring at the younger man, mumbling and growling, as he moved in for another round. He surprised Gabe when he feinted with his left, then brought a swooping right that caught Gabe on the side of his head, but Gabe had stepped back from the blow and turned his head, making the punch from Bernard a glancing one. Gabe saw lights dance before his eyes even from the near miss. Gabe quickly ducked under the expected left jab, brought his own left up from the ground and buried it in the big man's middle, driving him

back. He followed with a kick to his injured knee, and as
the big man stumbled, Gabe clasped his hands together and
brought down a driving chop to the back of the man's neck,
driving him to the ground.

Bernard rose to hands and knees, shaking his head and
scowled up at Gabe. He bellowed a roar as he rose and flashed
a knife in his hand as he charged. He held it low down, blade
up, and Gabe was quick to see this man had been in a few
knife fights before. He grabbed his own knife from the scabbard that hung between his shoulder blades and dropped
into a crouch, hands wide, knife flashing with the edge up.
Bernard said, "This is it boy, I'm the best knife man on the
Mississippi and I'm gonna gut'chu!" He lunged forward, but
Gabe side stepped and brought his knife up along the bottom
of the big man's forearm, drawing blood. Gabe stepped back
as Bernard reached to his arm with his free hand, brought it
back bloody and Gabe, standing relaxed as if he were waiting
for a servant to pour his tea, said, "Maybe you haven't noticed, but we're not on the Mississippi!"

The men came together like two enraged bulls, they
clashed horns and blades, each man grabbing the wrist of the
other. Bernard grinned, showing his rotten tobacco stained
teeth, what there were of them, and said, "Now, you're gonna
die boy!"

But Gabe gave way under the big man's lunge, dropping
as if he tripped, then used the momentum of the monster to
carry him over as he put his knee to his belly, his other leg
to his hip and threw the smelly Frenchman over his head, to

land flat of his back with an earth shaking thud. Gabe quickly came to his feet, dropped to his knees by the man's head and put the blade of his knife to his throat. "Who's gonna die?" he asked, glaring into the eyes of the beast. The big man tried to buck and come to his feet, but Gabe pressed down with the blade, drawing blood and making the man stop moving. Then he suddenly reached up and tried to grab Gabe by his hair, but the younger man slashed out with the knife, cutting the forearm of the man deeply, drawing blood that spurted and pumped. Bernard grabbed at the cut with his free hand, holding it high to see, unable to move out from under the blade that was once again at his throat.

Gabe had snatched up the dropped knife of Bernard and now loosely held the spare blade in his left hand, unknown to Bernard. He let up on the pressure of the blade at Bernard's throat, taunting the big man. Suddenly the hairy stump of the Frenchman flashed toward Gabe's head, but Gabe used the knife in his free hand to slash at the limb, cutting it as badly as the other. Bernard screamed, "You cut me! Both my arms! I'm gonna bleed to death! Help me!" The terror of the Mississippi was scared, facing death on his back in the dirt, with what he thought of as a pup of a man holding a knife at his throat.

Again he arched his back and kicked to try to buck off his assailant, and Gabe willingly stepped back, quickly drawing the razor edge of his knife across the man's throat. Bernard jumped to his feet, but his hand went to his throat and he felt the warm blood coursing over his hand. He looked up at Gabe, eyes wide with fear, and stumbled forward. He tried to speak but choked on his own blood as he staggered closer. Gabe sliced first with his knife, laying open the man's tunic and chest, then with the other and cut a big 'X' across his midriff, opening his gut wall. Bernard grabbed at his stomach, lifted his eyes to Gabe as he stumbled another step, then dropped to his knees. The impact split his gut and his intestines spilled out into his hands. He lifted his eyes to Gabe, and slowly fell forward on his face, splattering his own guts.

Gabe bent down and wiped the blades clean on the dirty tunic of the smelly Frenchman who would never harm another woman or child. Movement caught his eye and the Indian girl stepped closer and spat on the body of her captor. One eye was bruised, bleeding and swollen shut, the other cheek was blue and red and puffy. Her hair had a patch that had been ripped out, leaving a small bald and bleeding spot. Her tunic had been ripped and she struggled to keep it up at her shoulder. She stepped back, nose wrinkling, and looked at Gabe, then ran towards him, wrapped her arms around his waist and hugged him as she sobbed into his buckskins.

Turkey buzzards were already circling when they rode from the trees. A pair of coyotes disappeared into the trees and a badger came from his burrow. All were anticipating fresh meat for their dinner as Gabe and the girl rode side by side away from the small river known as the West Fork of the Little Sioux. They would be back with the others before dusk and Gabe was tired, tired of blood, tired of fighting, tired of riding, just plain tired. A good night's rest was what he looked forward to, maybe tonight.

11 / Omaha

As they rode, Gabe snatched a glance at the girl, frowning and shaking his head. Although he hadn't looked at the captives very closely, most of his time was spent with Wolf and Walking Bird, but he thought the girls were all less than twelve summers. But this one, even though she was small, her figure filled out that tunic and her hair was longer than that of a young girl. It was also in long braids, and probably saved her from having more of it ripped out like that patch above her temple. There was something different about her tunic, the beading was of blue and white beads, with quills offsetting the design. Although he had not been with the Pawnee long, this pattern of beading and quills was different somehow.

Although their path was ample enough for them to ride side by side, the girl stayed slightly behind Gabe, keeping her gaze down and never looking him in the eyes. It was almost two hours before they came to the Big Muddy and when they stopped atop the bank, Gabe stepped down and offered to help her down, but she slid off and to her feet. He gave her a quick glance and he asked, "Are you alright?" He spoke in English but used sign as well and she responded in her tongue which Gabe recognized to be much like that of the Osage. He was surprised because Wolf had never used that dialect when they spoke. He answered her in the language he learned while with the Osage, "You speak Osage?"

She frowned, her eyes squinting as she turned her head slightly, "No, I speak in the language of my people, the U-Mo'n-Ho'n, or as others say, the Omaha!"

"The Omaha? Aren't you one of the captives from the Pawnee village?"

She scowled, "I do not know the Pawnee."

He leaned one arm on the rump of Ebony, looked at her and asked, "When were you taken by that man?"

"Today! I was there," she pointed to the far bank, "I had some snares out for rabbits and he came off the bank on his horse, running, reached down and grabbed me and we crossed the river. He held me by my hair, and I tried to get away, but he was too big," she declared, stomping her foot. "But you came and killed him. Now I am indebted to you. My father is Black Cloud, the holy man of my people, my mother is White Elk Woman and my mother's father is Blackbird, the chief of all the Omaha. You must come with me to my village to help me tell of my capture."

He stood looking at her, amazed at her story, and paused, "I will go with you, but first, we must stop off and get my

friend." He pointed toward the tree covered bluff, "He's waiting for me yonder. We've got a couple packhorses and there's
some other women that the man back there," nodding with
his head back toward the scene of the fight, "took from the
Pawnee village."

As they rode up to the camp of the women, Ezra walked
toward him, cradling his rifle in his arms and looking at his
friend, "How is it that you take off after a big ugly Frenchman
and come back with a little bitty Indian woman?"

"Darned if I know. At first, I thought she was one o' these,"
nodding toward the Pawnee woman and children, "but come
to find out, she's from that big village yonder," nodding toward the previously seen village of the Omaha. "Her name
is Running Fox," started Gabe, turning in his saddle to
point to her, but she had already slid off the horse and was
talking in sign with Blue Flower and the girls. He saw where
she was, shook his head, and stepped down beside Ezra.
"Say, I was wonderin' when I was on the chase, about that
other one of the slavers. Weren't there two we left with
Wolf and his woman?"

"Now's a fine time to be wonderin'. For all you know,
he coulda been layin' out there in the woods with me in his
sights while you went galavantin' all over the countryside,
pickin' up stray women!" chided Ezra, grinning.

"Well, what happened with him?"

"I don't rightly know. Blue Flower don't talk much, but
we drug five bodies o'er to that gully yonder and caved

the bank over 'em. That was after we buried Wolf and his woman o'er by them trees. They had done somethin' awful to them bodies and I couldn't tell which was that last feller, but I left muh breakfast with 'em."

Running Fox came back to the side of Gabe, now standing beside Ezra, looked at Ezra with a frown, then reached for his hand, lifted it, rubbed her finger on the back of his hand, then dropped it and cocked her head slightly as she looked at Ezra again. She turned to Gabe, "I said the women could come to my village and we would help them, but they say they have guns and horses and goods and will go back to their people."

Gabe looked to Ezra and both men walked over to where Blue Flower sat with the girls and the young man, Badger. He asked, "You're plannin' on going back, alone?" He used sign with his limited skill in the Pawnee language to make himself understood. Blue Flower answered, "We," pointing with her chin toward Badger, "have the guns of the men that took us and we have horses and other goods. We will return."

"Well, we," motioning toward Ezra, "were plannin' on taking you back to your village. But first, I need to go to the Omaha village with Running Fox. If you can wait a day or two, we'll go back with you."

"There is no need. You have done enough in helping us to be free of those men. If you had not come, we would probably soon be dead. We are grateful, but we must return to our people."

Gabe, even with his limited experience with women,

knew better than to argue with one that had her mind made up. He knew she would probably see it as an affront for him to insist they accompany them, and he acceded to her decision. Within the hour, the six were on their way, led by Blue Flower and Badger, and trailing the two packhorses loaded with the goods and spare guns of the slavers.

When Gabe, Ezra and Running Fox approached the Omaha village, she began to explain to the men about the *Huthuga,* or the circular layout of the village. The north half of the lodges housed those that were known as sky people, the *Insta'shunda,* and the south half held the earth people, the *Hon'gashenu.* "Mine are the sky people and our lodge is in the first circle."

"How many are in your lodge?" asked Gabe.

Fox looked at the man with a frown, "All of my family," she answered, as if it was something everyone should already understand.

"Of course, I should have known that," muttered Gabe in English, just loud enough for Ezra to hear and chuckle.

Several lodges showed no activity and most of the people they saw were elderly or very young. Gabe looked at Running Fox and asked, "Are your people gone from the village?"

She turned to look at him and answered, "Most of the people have gone on the hunt in the time of greening. They went in three groups to hunt in different parts of the land. We are so many; it would be difficult for all the hunters and their families to make one hunt."

Some of the people came near and showed their concern by their expressions and greeting to Running Fox. Her injuries were evident and these strange men she was with were unknown by the people. The women, most elderly, stood back near the entrances to their sod roofed lodges, but some of the men walked alongside, a few carrying lances.

As Running Fox neared the lodge of her people, she saw some of her family come out of the entry way and stand, looking, frowns on their faces. Running Fox called out to them as she urged her horse closer and quickly dropped to the ground to run to her mother and embrace her. When she stepped back, she was peppered with questions and held up her hands to quiet her family members and began to explain. "I was checking my snares when a smelly Frenchman, suddenly rode up, reached down and grabbed me by my hair," she pointed to the spot on her head, "and threw me over his horse. I kicked and screamed but he kept hitting me. When we got to the little river, he stopped and threw me on the ground, made me get wood and start a fire. Then he came at me, hitting me again and again, and I screamed and kicked, but he was too big. He tore my tunic," she lifted the torn shoulder strap to show the listeners, "and started to do more but this man," pointing to Gabe, "hit him then beat him and killed him!" She walked back to put her hand on Gabe's leg, "He saved me," Running Fox explained and looked up at him with big adoring eyes.

"Were they together before they fought?" asked the older man, standing with arms folded across his chest. He was an impressive figure and his stance showed his authority and confidence.

Running Fox looked to Gabe and explained, "He is Blackbird, my grandfather and the chief of all the Omaha." She turned to answer, "No, grandfather, these men," motioning to Ezra, "were together and had rescued some Pawnee women and children from the man and his band. They killed them all and the Pawnee have gone back to their village."

Blackbird lifted his head slightly and dropped his arms to his side, then motioned and spoke, "Step down. You are welcome in our village. We are grateful for what you have done."

Gabe and Ezra stepped down and with reins in hand, he said, "I am called Gabe, and he," motioning to his friend, "is called Ezra. We thank you for the offer to stay, but we only wanted to bring Running Fox safely home. We will go now."

Running Fox stepped toward him, obviously agitated, and pleaded, "No, you must not go. It would be an insult to our chief for you to refuse his offer. We will have a meal, you can stay at least for the night, and then go."

Gabe glanced at the chief, saw the frown and turned to Ezra, "Looks like were stayin' for supper," and received a smile from his friend.

"Hey, that's fine by me. You know I like everybody's cookin' but my own." Gabe chuckled and turned back to Running Fox, looked to the chief and said, "It would be an honor to stay with your people."

The chief nodded and returned to his lodge. The women,

apparently the mother and grandmother of Running Fox smiled and nodded toward the friends. Running Fox said, "This is my mother, White Elk Woman, and my grandmother, Blood on her Hands."

Both Gabe and Ezra nodded to the women, and Gabe said, "Good to meet you ladies." Then turning to Running Fox asked, "Where should we put our horses and where do you want us to go?"

She smiled and said, "Follow me."

12 / Village

Gabe guessed the lodge to be about thirty feet in diameter. At the center was a fire pit, slightly sunken and lined with stones. Twelve posts, about six feet apart, outlined the center circle, which was about four feet below ground level, with beams reaching out to support the roof. A series of smaller poles lay between the support posts and cross beams to hold the roof in place. The outer circumference of the lodge was supported by posts every four to six feet. The outer circle roof was the same as the inner, but the outer ring held a shelf with storage areas underneath, that was used for beds and private areas closed off with hanging blankets and hides, giving each couple their privacy. The entry was a short passageway similar to a tunnel and faced the east. Gabe was reminded of the long houses of the natives of the Iroquois Confederacy in the northeast, having visited a village with his father shortly after the Revolutionary War.

Running Fox led them farther into the lodge and directed

them to an unused area behind a painted hide for them to put
their gear and where they would sleep. Fox waited for them
by the fire, motioned for them to be seated and explained,
"The others will be here soon, Blackbird will be seated there,"
motioning to the seat directly opposite the entry, "and the
others will be around the circle. You are in an honored place
to face the chief." She returned to the side of her mother and
assisted in the final preparations of the meal.

Blackbird and those nearest him acted as if Gabe and Ezra
were not even present during the meal. As with most meals
there was the usual chit-chat among those that were used to
being together as a family group, but Gabe and Ezra were
isolated, even though Running Fox tended to their every
need. Once the meal was over and the women had cleared
things away, Blackbird turned toward the visitors and asked,
"What is it you do? Are you trappers?"

Gabe answered, "No, we are not trappers. We do a little
trading now and then, but mostly we are just wanting to
explore the wilderness to the west."

"Do you not have a home and a woman?" he asked, leaning forward and frowning.

Gabe dropped his gaze, chuckled, then answered, "Yes.
We have homes. But those homes are of our fathers. We,"
motioning to Ezra and himself, "do not have any women,
nor have we built our own homes, yet. We want to learn of
the country and its people, like the Omaha, Pawnee, Otoe
and others."

The chief looked at Gabe, then at Ezra, and asked, "Why is he like the buffalo?"

Gabe looked at Ezra, grinning, "You wanna answer that?"

Ezra twisted around in his seat, looked at the chief, "Do you mean because I am the color of the buffalo?"

"Ummmhummm," answered the chief, nodding, but continued, "And your scalp, is like the head of the buffalo." He motioned to the holy man, Black Cloud, who was Fox's father and the man got up and went to his compartment at the edge of the lodge, returning with something under his arm.

Ezra felt his hair, grinned and glanced to Gabe, then looked at the chief. Black Cloud handed him a buffalo skull headdress that had the horns and thick hair of the buffalo. The chief pointed to the hair between the horns, then to Ezra's head, and nodded. Ezra grinned, "I guess it is a lot alike. Never thought of that before." He rubbed his hand over his thick curly scalp. "I take it you never saw a black man like me before, that right?"

"My grandfather told of those that were dark that came from the south with horses and metal bonnets and chests," he beat his fist against his chest to emphasize his point. "Their hair was dark like mine, but not like yours."

"Those must be the conquistadors of Spain that came before," suggested Gabe.

"Show me," ordered the chief, pointing at his own bare chest and then at Ezra.

Ezra frowned, not understanding, then Gabe chuckled, said, "He wants to see if you're black all over."

Ezra shook his head, stood and removed his buckskin tunic, then stripped down his faded red union suit, letting it hang at his waist. The chief and others stared, not just because he was darker than they, but he literally bulged with muscles. Ezra was not as tall as Gabe, yet his massive upper arms and shoulders rivaled most men's thighs, and his broad shoulders did little to frame his bulbous chest, and he didn't hesitate to flex his muscles to show them off. His torso tapered to a narrow waist, but his stomach was layered with muscles that crowded out any pretense of fat. Seldom would one see a man so developed as to be the envy of most other men. Gabe had always known Ezra to be strong, or as some would say, 'strong as an ox', but his loose-fitting tunic showed only that he was a big man. This showed he wasn't just big, he was muscular and undoubtedly strong. The entire room had gone silent as everyone stared, until Ezra began slipping his union suit over his shoulders and shrugged into his tunic.

"Is it true that the whites make slaves of your people?" asked the holy man, Black Cloud.

"Yes, that is true. Many of my people have been made slaves, but there are plenty of us who are not. My family lives free in Philadelphia as do many others. My father is a holy man, like you, and there are many that come to his church," and he thought of the word church and explained, "or village where he teaches."

"Your people, are they many?" asked the chief.

Ezra's shoulders slumped as he sat down, thinking, and then responded, "When you say 'my people' you probably mean those that are like me," he pointed to his cheek and hair, "and there are many. But we are not like the natives. You have the Osage, the Pawnee, the Omaha and others. All of you are the same, your skin and hair, but you are not the same people. With us, we have no tribes or differences, and we have no leaders of the many that are together in one place."

"You should be chief, lead your people, no longer be slaves," suggested Blackbird.

Ezra sighed heavily and forced a grin, "I wish it was that easy, chief. There have been times one or another has stood up and tried to lead, but they're always put down or killed. Perhaps someday it will be different."

The rest of the evening they talked of the surrounding country and other tribes. Most of the tribes were familiar, at least in name, to the men, Ponca, Kiowa, Comanche, Arapaho and Sioux. Gabe and Ezra were not familiar with Jicarilla and Mescalero Apache, and the Navajo. They also knew their knowledge of the many tribes was very limited. Although Blackbird spoke of some, the Ponca, Pawnee, Sioux, that they were friendly with, he also cautioned that a tribe's loyalties could change with the leadership.

With the rest of the conversation focused on the geography of the area, they spoke of well-known trails used by the Omaha people to go to the lands for their buffalo hunts. The men learned of prairies, plains, hills, rivers and more, but little was said about mountains, at least the mountains known as the Rockies. None of those present had been west far enough to see the mountains. Gabe said, "My father had a fellow officer in the war that told of an old man who had seen them and he called them the *pillars of heaven,* a phrase taken from the Bible."

The chief and others looked at him, frowning, glancing to one another, and the chief said, "My grandfather told of those that came with metal on their chests and head and they said there was a place where the sun sets that they called the pillars of heaven."

Ezra said, "That's from Job where he describes what God does, my Pa taught that, had me memorize it." He looked down, thinking, and as he started his eyes narrowed and he remembered his father, then said, "He stretcheth out the north over the empty place and hangeth the earth upon nothing. He bindeth up the waters in his thick clouds . . . he hath compassed the waters with bounds . . . the pillars of heaven tremble, and are admonished at his reproof . . . but the thunder of his power who can understand?" He opened his eyes wide, dropped his gaze and mumbled, "I think I forgot some of it, but that's most of it. It's from Job chapter 26."

The men of the lodge looked from one to another then to Ezra and Black Cloud asked, "Are you not a holy man also?"

Ezra chuckled, "No, no, I'm not a holy man."

"But you speak of your God in that way. He is what we call *Umon'-hon'ti.* He was before the *Insta'shunda* or Sky People and the *Hon'gashenu* or Earth People."

Ezra nodded, "Yes, we believe God was before all people. He created everything, then he created man and woman to tend his creation."

Black Cloud smiled, nodding, and although he sat with his legs crossed, he waddled just a little closer, and said, "Yes, it is so!" He turned to look at Blackbird, nodding and smiling, "I knew there was much we could agree with, this is a good thing to learn."

He stood and motioned for Ezra to follow him and the two walked from the lodge with Black Cloud talking very animatedly and Ezra nodding and listening. Blackbird and the others also rose as did Gabe, chuckling as he watched the two men leave the lodge.

Running Fox came to Gabe's side, "I have prepared your beds for you. Is there anything else I can do?" she smiled up at her liberator, showing a coquettish smile.

Gabe, somewhat befuddled at her behavior stammered, "Uh, uh, thanks, but no, there's nothing for you to do. I'll, uh, just go to my blankets, I'm kinda tired," he explained, trying to get away, yet sneaking a look toward Fox's mother and father, neither of whom were paying any attention to Fox. He knew the native people had different beliefs of the way of men and women, but regardless of their beliefs, his belief was that he wasn't interested in any man/woman behavior of any kind.

He backed away from Fox, she followed smiling, but he found the painted hide that shielded his sleeping area and ducked behind it. That did not deter the girl as she followed him into the private area. Gabe turned to see the blankets had been layed with a wide spread of blankets covering a thick buffalo robe, ample space for more than one, with another smaller layout of blankets below the shelf, and to the side. Fox saw him look at the smaller pallet and explained, "That is for your friend, Ezra."

"And this?" asked Gabe, motioning to the larger layout of blankets at his side.

"For us."

The next almost one hour was spent with Gabe trying to exercise every bit of diplomacy and conversational etiquette in explaining to Running Fox that although she was a very beautiful and desirable woman, there could be no 'us' because of his beliefs and that of his family. He wasn't sure whether or not she totally understood or agreed, but she finally left. Ezra just happened to return as she was leaving the sleeping area and he looked at Gabe with a question on his face, but understood when he saw Gabe sitting, head hanging in his hands, shaking his head.

Ezra chuckled and asked, "Did you get us into more trouble, again?"

13 / Getaway

Black Cloud scratched on the hide, then pushed it aside and stepped into the small sleeping area of the two men. Both looked up expectantly and Gabe said, "Black Cloud, something you need?"

The medicine man stepped to the edge of the sleeping shelf and seated himself near Ezra, leaned over to look at Gabe and said, "I must speak to you of Running Fox."

"Black Cloud, I told her she was not to be with me. I explained that I am not ready to take a woman to my lodge. She said she understood," replied Gabe, apprehensively.

"Yes, I know. But she is a woman who does what she wants. She told her mother she was going with you."

Gabe leaned back slightly, holding his open palms before him, and said, "Whoa. I did not tell her to come with us. She needs to stay here with her people," responded Gabe, eyebrows lifted, and chin tucked toward his chest.

Black Cloud grinned, "I know. She says she will guide you through the land of the Ponca and if you still do not want her, she will return with the people of our village that went on the first hunt for the buffalo."

"Is that what you want, Black Cloud?" asked Gabe, hoping for a negative answer but afraid of just the opposite.

"You must pay for her. I will not take less than one rifle, one hand-gun, powder and balls, two blankets, and beads for my woman," he stood, stoic before the two friends.

"Whoa, I thought you didn't want her to go!?" pleaded Gabe, growing a little frantic.

"She has decided. She will go. You must pay," declared the medicine man.

"And if I don't pay?"

"I command the warriors. They will take you and every-thing you have. Then they will take your life."

Gabe slumped back on the sleeping robe, shaking his head as Ezra said, "I knew it! I knew it! Just like I figgered, more trouble!" He looked to his friend, "So, what'cha gonna do?"

Gabe frowned at Ezra then turned to Black Cloud, "What if she decides to come back with your hunting party? Do I get my goods back?"

"No," answered Black Cloud, now with arms folded across his chest and grinning.

Gabe shook his head, sat up, looked at the apathetic Indian leader and said, "So, it's a little or everything." He looked at Ezra and asked, "What're we gonna do with an Indian girl?"

"Not my problem," chuckled Ezra. "But we know she can

cook!" and smiled at his friend.

Gabe and Ezra rolled out of their blankets early, the only light coming from the dying embers of the cookfire. Last night after their dicker with Black Cloud, they had stacked their gear outside, ready for the coming journey. Gabe had a little hope that they might be able to leave without Running Fox and they stealthily left the lodge, dropping the blanket at the entrance to mask any sound of their packing. Ezra had gone to fetch the horses and was leading the four animals to the lodge when Gabe stepped from the entry.

Nary a word passed between them as they saddled their mounts and rigged the packs on the packhorses. With one last check, a nod of the head and they swung aboard the horses, grinning and believing they would make their getaway. Though he had given in to the demand of Black Cloud on the trade goods, Gabe thought it a small price for freedom. They kicked their horses forward to the passageway from the village and approached the edge of the many lodges, excited to be back on the trail. They were stopped by Running Fox, sitting astride her paint pony, a blanket roll behind her, another one across the pommel of her saddle. She was smiling broadly and waited for the two to draw up beside her. She said, "I am happy to go with you," then reined her mount around to take the lead and started on the trail that led away from the west edge of the village, the thin grey line that separated the darkness of the night from the shadowy earth at their backs.Little was said as the three traveled, any

conversation was between Ezra and Gabe and about incon-
sequential matters. They enjoyed the prairie with its tall
grasses, bluestem and Indian grass mostly, all growing belly
high on the horses. The lush green stretched beyond the
limits of their eyesight and was only broken by a smattering
of trees that lined some marshland or creek bottom. It was a
radical change from the forested hills east of the Mississippi
River and often prompted the explorers to stand in their
stirrups and shade their eyes to search for anything in the
distance that told of a change in the terrain. After one such
stretch, Gabe turned to Ezra, "Isn't it a wonder? This country
is so vast it makes me feel like a little insignificant creature!"

Ezra was quiet a moment then answered, "Nope, nope,
you're looking at things wrong, my friend. Instead of thinking
how little you are, think of how big God is that he stood upon
nothing and created everything! I remember my Pa preaching
from Psalms, chapter nineteen, I think. 'The heavens declare
the glory of God; and the firmament showeth his handiwork.'"

Gabe looked all around, sighed heavily, "Yup, reckon
you're right. His handiwork sure is somethin' and I'm thinkin'
it's gonna just get better and better. I remember seeing some
early paintings and sketches of the Alps, over in Europe,
and I thought they were amazing but I'm thinking we've got
some mighty big mountains in the Rockies just waiting for
us to explore. And I'm pretty sure they're gonna be ever bit
as impressive as the Alps!"

"So, you think we'll be the first ones to explore the Rockies?" asked Ezra.

Gabe chuckled, "Nope, that's already been done by Alexander Mackenzie, 'bout three, four years ago, but he crossed the Rockies way up north. As far as I know, the only ones, other than the natives of course, that have explored the Rockies were some of the Conquistadors and French *coureurs des bois,* maybe some Spaniards. Probably been some trappers of all sorts but nothing has been recorded as a particular exploration mission or such like."

The two men, as boys, had often talked and shared dreams and hopes of what it would be like to be explorers and discover new lands. While Gabe took advantage of every opportunity for education and study of the unexplored lands, Ezra was tasked with helping his family. With his father the pastor of the Mother Bethel African Methodist Episcopal Church in Philadelphia, he had little time for the usual duties at home and those tasks fell upon the shoulders of Ezra. Yet from their adolescent years until they grew to manhood, the two had been friends and took every opportunity to spend time in the woods, sharpening their skills at hunting, fishing, and exploring. Those shared dreams had helped to shape the boys into men and the skills learned in the forests of Pennsylvania were the foundation blocks of their wilderness knowledge.

Yet the molding and shaping of a man's character is begun early, with teaching and examples from their families. Both boys had lost their mothers in their early teen years and learned to lean on their fathers more than that of the usual young man.

Gabe's father was a man of many talents in the business

world and had amassed a considerable fortune with his investments and business dealings, never tying himself down to one particular business, but helping others to succeed by investing in their ventures and enriching himself as well. He was known as a man of exceptional character, always honest and forthright in his dealings, traits he passed on to his only son.

Ezra's father was a man of faith, an avid student of the Bible and with a heart to minister to his fellow man. Although he hoped Ezra would enter the ministry, he taught the young man about character, wisdom, and faith in the God of all creation, and always encouraged him to follow his heart. Now the traits of the two men melded together as their bond of friendship and brotherhood grew, friends that could always depend on one another. With that lifelong friendship came a kinship that enabled the two men to know as much and sometimes more about the other as he knew himself, resulting in their ability to anticipate the other's actions or thoughts unerringly. This was a trait that had already served them well and more than once saved their lives.

A slight rise in the terrain gave the riders a view of the flat land before them and Running Fox pointed to a line of dark green, "There is water." She lifted her eyes to the western horizon that cradled the lowering sun and asked, "Do you want to stop?" Although these had been the only words spoken by the woman since they left her village, her countenance had shown no emotion, but her eyes showed excitement, and a glimmer of happiness. She let a slow smile cross her face as she lowered her eyes from Gabe, awaiting his answer.

He shook his head, trying to rid his mind of the negativity that came whenever he thought of her subterfuge that brought her here. He had to admit, she was an exceptionally beautiful woman. He thought to himself that he probably should be flattered that a woman such as this would go to such lengths to be with him, but it still grated that he had little say in the matter, even after going to great pains to explain to her they couldn't be together. He sighed and nodded, "Yeah, we should make camp and that looks like the best place around." She smiled, nodded, and kicked her horse forward to lead the way to the trees clustered at the riverbank.

While the men tended the horses, Fox busied herself with gathering firewood and readying the cookfire. Gabe noted her carefulness in selecting a site for the fire, ensuring the ring of stones around the flames were sufficient to block the glare and the placement under the outstretched limbs of a massive bur oak that would dissipate any smoke. When the men were finished with the horses and gear, they were surprised to see the coffee pot dancing on a flat stone near the flames and emitting the enticing aroma of the black brew. Fox had fashioned a tripod of green sticks that suspended the pot over the fire from which came the aroma of some stew. A pan at the side of the fire held some type of biscuits and the entire meal was tantalizing the men with their ravenous appetites.

Ezra looked to Gabe, winked and nodded, "Ummhumm, maybe she ain't so much trouble after all."

"Hummph," was the only answer offered by Gabe as he plopped down beside the fire.

14 / Storm

For the next two days, the mood of the travelers was unchanged. Running Fox maintained her serene manner, cheerfully assuming the duties of cooking and more. If her mood changed from tranquil it was usually to a more cheerful and somewhat contagious manner. As they rode, she would often stop and gather hands full of plants, roots, and even blossoms to add to the evening's fare. They didn't lack for variety and after Ezra showed her how to fix Johnny cakes, he was even happier. Never one to refuse food of just about any kind, he especially enjoyed the Johnny cakes, or with a little variety, corn dodgers. She kept to her own blankets but was always near Gabe often anticipating his needs or wants when it came to food or camp duties. He didn't want to admit it, but she was growing on him.

Early afternoon on the third day out of the Omaha village, the grey bottom clouds brought the threat of a spring storm. Wherever they looked, there was nothing but the beginning of rolling hills and no cover offered. Fox stood in her stirrups and pointed, "There!" In the distance was a cluster of trees at what appeared to be a bend in a creek or river. With a quick glance to the clouds, the three kicked their mounts to a canter, hoping to reach cover before the bottom fell out of the storm clouds.

Skidding to a stop under the tall hickory and hackberry cluster, Gabe grabbed for the ground covers while Ezra picked a pair of trees and began cutting a sapling that was long enough to stretch between the two. Within moments, Fox had carried several limbs and long branches to stack along the stripped sapling to form the lean-to. Gabe stretched one of the oiled ground covers across the branches, another underneath, and then assisted Fox in laying more over the cover.

Once the lean-to was ready, Fox scurried around, gathering dry firewood and stacking it near the fire ring she made with the nearby rocks. Ezra had stacked the gear under a close in tree with thick foliage, hoping for enough protection for the saddles and packs. Gabe tended the horses, picketing them in the thick cluster of silver maple and redbud that offered a good windbreak and shelter under the wide spreading branches.

With all their scampering around, they paid little attention to the impending storm, but the sudden roll of thunder followed by lances of lightning that split the sky, they knew they were in for it. The fire was blazing, and the coffee pot was on when the first drops of rain rattled the leaves like the drum roll of a marching corps. The big drops pelted the men as they finished their preparations, and the fire hissed its protests with each splatter of water. They had stretched out their bedrolls in the lean-to and now found a seat on the edge, just under the overhang of the shelter. Fox tended the last of the pork belly in the frying pan while she finished mixing the dough for the corn dodgers. Gabe and Ezra sat silently, watching, and letting their minds wander. The deep growl of the thunder shook the ground and rattled the tree branches, but the crackle and hiss of the lightning that struck nearby made the three of them jump and stare. Again and again the lightening hit, walking ever nearer with each strike. When it struck so close they saw the tree across the way split with the blow and the blast was so loud the horses jerked at their tethers, the men came from the shelter, looking everywhere, hoping the storm would soon slacken.

Then suddenly, making time stand still, a many tongued lance of lightning struck a towering black walnut tree split-ting it from the tallest branch to the ground. The shards of lightning sent sparks, splintered wood, bark and dirt flying in every direction. The nearby trees swayed with the blast of the bolts and the static climbed the legs and arms of all three that stood mesmerized by the fire. A sudden deluge snuffed the fire, soaking the corn dodgers and splattering the grease from the pork belly.

The shock of the blast startled the horses and they pulled free from the pickets, fleeing through the trees and into the grasslands. Gabe looked back at the lightning struck tree, hollered a warning and grabbed Running Fox and dove under the massive hickory tree that sheltered the gear. The split walnut trunk slowly bent apart, and the big tree splattered to the ground in three directions with the tallest portion splitting the sapling over the lean-to and burying the bedrolls in the thick greenery. Ezra turned to Gabe, held up the coffee pot, "Well, at least we got coffee!"

Shaking his head, Gabe looked at his friend, then to Fox and asked, "Everybody alright?"

Both Fox and Ezra nodded, freeing Gabe to dig in their gear for some of the remaining trade blankets and a handful smoked meat for their meal. He mumbled, "Guess it could be worse." The smell of lightning hung in the trees, reminding them how close they had come to being crushed beneath the massive walnut tree. They huddled together, sharing the blankets and body heat, and in time, got a little sleep.

The crashing of the storm-fed stream carrying the debris from the cloudburst brought the three awake. The dim grey light of early morning stared into their faces as they struggled from the tangle of blankets and gear. Fox stood and stretched, glanced at the water of the stream licking at the grass nearby, then disappeared into the trees. Neither Gabe nor Ezra could stand under the low hanging limbs and had to hunker down in a crouch to come from under the big tree.

They stood together, looking at the storm damage, then agreed their first task would be to fetch the horses back. "How 'bout I go after the horses, you get our stuff from under that tree, maybe start another fire."

"Don't you want your rifle?" asked Ezra, knowing their long guns were in the shelter.

"Nah, I'll take a saddle pistol and my bow. Maybe I'll even get us some fresh meat!" he suggested, returning under the low branches to retrieve his weapons.

Horses are herd animals and Gabe was confident he would find Ebony and the others close together, knowing they would have found shelter and Ebony as the herd stallion, would keep them together. From their first day together, Gabe would always whistle whenever he came to feed the big black. The same whistle had called the horse from the far pasture many times and the close bond between man and horse always brought them together.

As he neared the edge of the trees, he started his two-toned whistle, looking and listening for an answering whinny. When he broke from the trees, he stopped and searched the flats beyond, but there was no sign of the horses. The storm had obliterated the tracks from the animals and the only thing he had to go on was the direction they fled from their camp. He started off, holding close to the tree line, whistling often and waiting for an answer, but none came.

He had been on the search since first light, and it was approaching mid-morning and still no sign. He spotted a snag of a big cottonwood, shimmied up the grey hulk and used the height to scan the nearby terrain. There was no movement, save the sway of the tall grasses in the morning breeze. He looked down for a stub of a branch to start his descent and something caught his eye. He paused, looked to the rolling hills to the northwest and movement snared his attention. There, just below the shoulder of that bald knob, it looked like Fox's little paint mare. Her head was down in the belly-high grass, but suddenly it came up, ears forward and nose stretched out. Something had alarmed her, but she didn't move away, just stood watching. Maybe the other horses were on the far side of that knob.

Gabe slipped quickly down and started at a long stride trot toward the paint. He was wet from his waist down with the rain-soaked grasses, but he kept his pace, letting a whistle cut the air, hopeful of hearing Ebony's answer. He kept his pace until nearing the knob, then slowed, caught his breath and climbed the hill, anticipating seeing the four other horses on the far side. As Gabe topped the ridge, he was shocked to see many horses and at the edge of the herd, Ebony.

The big stallion was rearing up, pawing the air and baring his teeth as he fought against two young men with rawhide ropes, trying to capture the black horse. He dropped to all fours, stretched out his head, ears back, teeth bared and chased one of the Indians away from the herd. He spun around, looking for another and seeing the second man swinging his rope overhead, he reared up again, pawing and neighing in a screaming cry of defiance and as the young man threw his loop Ebony's hoof knocked it down and he dropped into a charge, trying to take a bite out of the fleeing youngster.

Both of the Indians stood far back from the horses, and

another joined them. The three were talking animatedly, gesturing and arguing with one another. Gabe guessed the distance to be about two hundred yards and nocked an arrow, brought it to full draw and let it fly. He had chosen a special whistling arrow, one made with a bone arrowhead with hollowed channels that caused a multi-pitched whistle that sounded a little like a scream. The shaft whistled toward its mark, catching the attention of the boys who stood agape as it neared. They stood wide-eyed, transfixed, unable to spot the missile until it buried itself in the turf at their feet. The three jumped back, staring at the arrow, then looked to see where the shooter might be, but the only movement was of one man that walked down the slope of the small butte and was too far away to have sent an arrow that distance.

The boys were frozen with both fear and curiosity as they watched the tall man draw near. They continued to search the nearby area for another that might have sent the arrow, but there was no one. Gabe approached the three, greeted them with, "Aho!" as he raised one hand, palm forward. The boys were slow to answer but finally returned the greeting as the tall blonde white man in buckskins came close. They looked at him, then at the strange bow he held at his side and watched as he drew the arrow from the ground, examined it and slid it into the quiver at his side.

"Are these your horses?" asked Gabe, using the same language as the Omaha, together with sign. He gestured toward the herd and looked back at the boys.

The tallest and probably the oldest of the three stepped

forward, "These are the horses of our village," and pointed to the west. "We were sent for them."

Gabe nodded, "Some of them are ours. The big black stallion you were trying to catch is mine." He turned and sounded his whistle. Ebony lifted his head, nickered, and trotted to Gabe, head held high, mane and tail flying. When he came close, the three boys stepped back, wary. But Gabe held out his hand and the stallion dropped his head for Gabe's touch, accepting the affectionate rub on his face, and the arm around his neck.

"I am Gabe. This," nodding to Ebony, "is Ebony. There are three other horses there that belong to me, and that little paint yonder, too."

The speaker of the group answered, "He is a beautiful animal. My name is Standing Bear, and this is White Eagle and Crazy Wolf."

Gabe slipped the rawhide tether rope around Ebony's neck, grabbed a handful of mane and swung aboard. He looked down at the boys, "I'll just cut out my other horses and get back to my camp. We might come see your village in a day or so, you might tell your people to expect us." The three boys nodded, and watched the white man cut out the other horses and drive them back toward the long line of trees that marked the location of the small stream that fed the big river.

Ezra was standing at the tree line, rifle cradled in his arms, as he watched Gabe push the four horses into the trees. He looked at his friend, "What took you so long? I was about to head out to look for you!"

Gabe pointed to the horses with his chin, "They got mixed in with a herd from the village by the river. Three boys thought they'd try their hand at catching Ebony and he had to play with 'em for a while."

"Yeah, I can imagine. That big black doesn't play with anybody but you! What'd he do, take a hunk o' hide outta their hind ends?"

"No, but he was about to, but I got there in time to keep the peace. I don't think those boys will forget it, and they'll probably think twice 'fore they try to catch a wild horse again."

"Well, I'll get these four tethered, you better get you some o' that food your woman fixed 'fore it's all gone. She won't appreciate you missin' out!"

"My woman! She ain't my woman!" declared Gabe, spitting out the words.

Ezra chuckled, "She shore ain't mine!"

15 / Ponca

"Nanza!" declared Running Fox, pointing to the west across the Niobrara River. They sat atop a bald rise on the east side, overlooking the muddy waters of the Niobrara. The river was just over a hundred yards wide, this near the mouth and the confluence with the Missouri, but the minimal riffles showed shallow waters. Gabe was surprised to see a fortified village that resembled the military forts of the white man. With what Gabe guessed to be some sort of moat around the vertical post palisade that stood atop a berm, the many earthen lodges were well protected. He leaned forward on the pommel, looking at the unique site, and estimated thirty lodges were within the walls. He looked to Fox, "Tell me about that," pointing with his chin to the village.

Fox smiled, sitting back as she looked at Gabe, "This is Nanza, the village of the Ponca. It has been here since before the time of my grandfather. The legends are that the Ponca and the Omaha were one people, but these," nodding toward the village, "separated and made their own village. My people went downstream to make their village. But we have always been at peace with the Ponca, and we speak the same tongue."

"But the only Indian villages I've seen like this, with the walls and all, were a part of the Iroquois Confederacy, but even then, it wasn't as big as this," stated Gabe, wonder in his tone.

"You have seen these Iroquois people?" she asked, awed that anyone had seen the people she had only heard about in the old legends. Before Gabe could answer, she continued. "The old people tell the stories of how their grandfathers and their fathers before them lived beyond the big river, near lakes that were so big you could not see across them. The Iroquois drove our people from that land and we came to this place," related Fox, somberly. She lifted her eyes, and said, "We will go to the village. We had word there is a trader here that has many goods." Without waiting for a response, she stepped her horse toward the river, and without hesitating took to the water.

They dropped off the cut bank to cross the stream, then over a shoal before dropping into the current of the river. As expected, it wasn't even belly deep on the horses, but the long-legged Gabe's stirrups bobbed in the water now and then. They could tell by the struggling steps of the horses that the river bottom held considerable silt, but the animals kept their pace, up and over shallow islands, into the water, and again. It was a braided river they crossed, but it showed itself to be an easy crossing and they were soon climbing the low bank on the west side.

They stepped down to allow the horses their usual rolling shake, then remounted and started up the slight rise toward the village. It was situated on the shoulder of some rolling hills that appeared as a low ridge with timber growing on the north side, but bald on the south. In the lee of the long ridge was the village. Just over a hundred yards from the main entrance, sat a low roofed log cabin where several horses were tethered, and a handful of Ponca men lounged about. Fox started for the village entry, but Gabe asked, "I thought you wanted to go to the trader?"

She turned and spoke over her shoulder, "We must go to the village first, let the people know we are here and peaceful." Gabe slowly lifted his head in a nod and both men followed after the woman. As they rode into the village, several people watched, but none were concerned, perhaps because of the woman who rode before them. With the village arranged similar to what they had seen with the Omaha, Fox led them to the central compound where a couple of people were standing, waiting, having been told of the visitors. Fox stepped down, walked toward a line of men, obviously the leaders, and spoke to the man that stood slightly forward of the others.

"I am Running Fox of the *U-Mo'n-Ho'n*. My grandfather is Blackbird. These," motioning to Gabe and Ezra, "are friends of my people and the *P'anka iyé*. That one," pointing to Gabe, "is Gabe, and the other is Ezra." She turned to face

Gabe, "This is Buffalo Horn, the chief of the Ponca."

The chief motioned for them to dismount, and once aground, both men stepped forward, hands extended and the men clasped forearms, then stepped back. The chief looked at Gabe, then turned to look at a young man standing nearby. "He is not as big as you say." Gabe noticed the young man, remembering him as Standing Bear, one of the three boys with the horses. The chief turned back, "My son has told us of you and your horse. That is a beautiful animal, I would trade for him."

Gabe grinned and asked, "If he was yours, would you talk trade?"

The chief cast a somber gaze to Gabe, "No."

"Nor will I. He has been my friend for many years, since I was the age of your son," nodding toward Standing Bear.

"It is a wise man that knows a horse is more than a beast to ride." He frowned and looked at Gabe, "My son also said you shot an arrow that sings, and from a great distance. Is this so?"

"Your son speaks true," answered Gabe, simply.

The chief lifted his eyes to the sun, then back to Gabe. "We will eat, then you will show me this arrow that sings and flies so far."

Gabe looked directly at the chief, "It would be an honor to have a meal with you, but we must also make camp."

Buffalo Horn lifted a hand, "My son will take you to a lodge. You are welcome in our village for this night."

Gabe grinned, nodding, and at the motion from Standing

Bear, the three followed the young man to the lodge. They stripped the horses, tethered them beside the lodge, and placed their gear inside. Ezra asked, "Did you catch that when the chief said we are welcome for *this* night?"

Gabe chuckled, "Yeah, I did. Guess their hospitality is rather short-lived."

Fox interjected, "It is the custom with visitors to make them welcome for one night. If the chief should decide you are a good man, then more nights would be offered."

Gabe looked to Ezra, both men nodded as Ezra said, "Sounds reasonable."

"Ummhumm," agreed Gabe.

Gabe, Ezra and Fox enjoyed the meal in the lodge of Buffalo Horn, his wife and daughter tending to their guests. It soon became obvious that the chief was anxious to see this singing arrow and the bow that shoots so far, so much so that he cut the meal short and hurried everyone outside for the demonstration. Gabe went to their lodge, fetched the bow and quiver and returned. Buffalo Horn led the small enclave outside the village and stopped near the main entry. With the village situated atop the low rising flat-topped hills, below them lay the grass covered floodplain that held the trader's cabin and a horse herd grazing in the distance.

The chief looked to Gabe, "My son will take a hoop with a hide for you to use as your mark. Where do you want it?" He looked to the flood plain, waiting for Gabe to direct his son with the target.

Gabe looked at the target, then to the chief, "For you to hear the arrow that sings, put the hide there," he pointed to a bush near the palisade and no more than ten yards from where they stood. "I will go down there and shoot the arrow back here," suggested Gabe, pointing to the target.

The chief looked at the tall white man, frowning, then to the target and nodded his head. Gabe took off at a trot, having already chosen a spot for his shooting position. He stopped at a cluster of chokecherry and elderberry bushes, dropped to the ground and strung the bow. With the draw weight of the bow well over one hundred pounds, he placed his feet against the bow and pulled back on both limbs, nocking the string. He stood, looking at the target, now not much more than a bright dot about three hundred yards distant, and nocked his arrow. Before drawing, he placed one whistling arrow and another at his feet. Once ready, he lifted the bow, brought it to full draw with the jade thumb ring and let the first arrow fly. Before the first hit the target, the second and whistling arrow was on its way followed closely by the third arrow. Gabe threw the bow case over his shoulder and started at a trot back to the palisade.

The chief was accompanied by two other leaders of the village, his son, and his wife. Running Fox stood beside Ezra as they watched Gabe ready himself and his bow. When he stood, Ezra said, "Here comes the first arrow!" and watched as Gabe did as Ezra expected and fired three arrows. Because of the speed and distance, the arrows could not be easily seen and before the first hit the target, the attention of the spectators was grabbed by the whistling arrow as it sped toward the hide, but before it struck the target, the first arrow had thudded into the hide, almost dead center. Within seconds, the whistler also pierced the hide followed by the third and last arrow.

The chief was speechless as he looked from the archer in the distance and back to the hide stretched over the hoop and leaning against the brush. Only the fletching of the arrows was visible, the shafts having penetrated the hide and now were hidden by the brush. Chatter broke out among all the spectators with Standing Bear smirking and laughing at his father's incredulity. Bear looked at his father, "Is it not as I said? No one can shoot an arrow as far as this man, nor as fast and accurate!"

The two elders that stood by the chief walked to the target, touched the fletching on the arrows and leaned the target back to see the shafts and the arrowheads. They saw one was different and looked at it closely, recognizing it to be made of bone. "This is the one that made the sounds, see the holes?" said the grey-haired man called Black Elk.

The second elder, Spotted Horse, answered, "All the arrows are longer," pointing to the shafts and stretching out his fingers and palm to measure. "They are one hand longer than our arrows."

Both men stood and returned to the group who watched as Gabe trotted up to the target to remove his arrows. Once done, he dropped them into the quiver and walked to the side of Buffalo Horn. He withdrew the whistler, handed it to

Horn and pointed to the bone point, "That is bone, and the holes are what make it whistle."

Horn examined the arrow, returned it, then reached for the bow, which Gabe had extended toward him. The chief examined the weapon closely, fingering the laminate, the recurve, and the grip. He lifted it up, put his fingers to the string to draw and was surprised at how hard it was to even begin a draw. He released the string, frowned at Gabe, and said, "It is very strong!"

"Yes, that's stronger than two or three of the usual bow."

The chief look at his fingers, rubbing them with his thumb, then looked at Gabe's hand, saw the thumb ring and lifted his eyes to Gabe's in a question. Gabe chuckled, then demonstrated the pull by using his thumb with the ring on the string, looping his fingers over the thumb, then drew the bow to a full draw and slowly let it off.

The chief grinned, nodded, and said, "It is a strong bow. Can you use it on a buffalo hunt?"

"I have, yes. One arrow, here," pointing to his side below the shoulder, "will take down a buffalo."

"Will you show us how to make such a bow?" asked Buffalo Horn.

"I would, but it takes many moons to make one. Very difficult and the wood," he pointed at the heart of the laminate, "is not found here. The horn," pointing to the layer of ram's horn on the belly of the bow, "is from the bighorn sheep that is only found in the mountains."

"Will you trade for this bow? I will give you two hands of

horses," exclaimed the chief.

Gabe grinned, "No, Buffalo Horn, I cannot. We are going west to the Rockies and I am told there are bears there that stand as tall as two men and can kill a man with one swipe of his big paw. I need this bow to take one of those bear."

The chief recognized and appreciated the man and his purpose. He had the heart of a hunter and respected that in another man. Horn nodded and said, "You are a good man and wise to keep your horse and your weapon. We value friends like you."

16 / Resupply

"Ah, *mon ami, bien venu!* Welcome, welcome. You are British, no?" asked Jean Baptiste Munier, the trader granted a trading monopoly with the Ponca by the Spanish governor-general.

"No, we're American!" answered Gabe, rather curtly, frowning at the man.

"All the better! What brings you to this land?" asked the trader, trying to be friendly and hoping for a profitable trade with the man.

"Oh, we're just passing through. Headin' west to the Rockies."

"Ah, I understand, you are an *aventurier,* uh, an adventurer." He paused, smiling and looking around, "And what can I offer you today?"

Gabe began, "We need some powder, lead, sugar, flour, salt, and that'll do for starters."

"Uh, are you trading pelts or furs?" asked Munier.

"No, you'll take gold coin, won't you?"

"*Oui, oui,*" he answered, turning to begin filling the order.

They had spent the first few hours of the day trading with the Poncas for beans, corn, some buckskins and moccasins, and an additional pack horse. When the trader began filling the order, Ezra started carrying it out to start packing it away. Running Fox stood beside Gabe, watching every move of both Gabe and the trader until Gabe asked, "Anything you need?" motioning around to the shelves and stacked goods. She pointed at a paper of needles and smiled. Gabe turned back to the trader, "Better add four papers of needles, three awls, an assortment of beads, bells, and those geegaws over there. Six of those blankets," and he continued looking and considering. Once the order was complete, the trader added things up, gave the total, which was considerable, but pondering the alternatives, Gabe begrudgingly dug deeper and paid the man with coin.

The trader grinned, "We never see gold out here and these are so new!" he bit one to test the metal and grinned up at Gabe. "Merci, and good luck on your adventure!" Gabe nodded, gave a back-handed wave over his shoulder as he followed Fox from the cabin.

"How long will it be before we are out of the land of the Ponca?" asked Gabe, enjoying the ambling gait of the big black. They had traveled through the day and were nearing their first camp after leaving the big village of the Ponca. He was thinking about Fox's statement of guiding them through the land of the Ponca and then deciding to either stay with the men or return with her people as they came from the buffalo hunt.

"Our lands have no lines or fences like the white men. There is the understanding that certain places are of different people. For the Ponca, the place where two rivers come from the south together with this one called the Niobrara, the far river of the two is the place. That river is the land of the Lakota," answered Fox.

"And the Ponca and the Lakota are not friendly?" asked Ezra.

"No, but the Ponca, like the Omaha, have been at peace with those who live close."

Gabe had noticed that Fox had been a little reticent throughout the day and now was hesitant to express herself. He didn't want to intrude on her thoughts, but he was concerned. When people are isolated and few, it is easy for the mood of one to affect them all. He asked her, "Are you alright? You've been a little quiet today."

"This is the first I have been from my family," she answered somberly.

Gabe nodded, understanding, and said, "I know how you feel." He considered a moment how to express himself so she could understand and not misconstrue what he said, "It is not a good feeling when you miss your family. We call it being homesick. It's a feeling, here," pointing to his lower chest, "and thoughts here," pointing to his head, "about your family." He motioned to Ezra and himself, "We have felt this because we left our families and homes also."

Fox was sitting easy in the saddle, rocking with the gait of the horse, head down, staring at the trail glassy-eyed. She glanced toward Gabe, nodded her head, and reached down to stroke the neck of her horse. There is a kinship between a man or woman and their horse that breaches the chasm of loneliness and emptiness and Fox needed that closeness, the nearness of a friend that would not reproach and try to explain, but just feel and share. The paint pony turned its head back for just a moment and her head bobbed as if agreeing and empathizing. Gabe watched and a slight smile tugged at the corners of his mouth.

"Was there anyone else other than your mother and father?"

She lifted surprised eyes to Gabe, frowning slightly and quietly answered, "I had a friend, the son of the war-chief, *Padhin-nanpaji* or He-who-fears-not-the-sight-of-a-Pawnee, his name is Two Crows. We wanted to be together, for me to be his woman, but he did not have what my father asked from him for me to be his mate. He left on the buffalo hunt before you came."

Gabe smiled, suddenly hoping he had a way out of this complication he found himself in with Running Fox. "Where do they go on this hunt?"

Ezra had been riding lead and interrupted their conversation when he reined up and pointed to a meandering tree lined stream, "That looks like a good spot to make camp for the night, what say?" he asked as he looked back to Gabe.

"Looks good to me, and I am gettin' a little hungry," answered Gabe.

They fell into their routine of making camp and before long found themselves sitting back and enjoying the after-supper cup of coffee. Gabe asked Fox again, "You were about to tell me where your people went on their buffalo hunt, where is that?"

"When the buffalo move north in the time of greening, our people are led in three bands to hunt. They start in the south above the low branch of the Platte river. As the herd is driven north by the hunters, the next band will be waiting above the longer branches of the river. The last band is hunting farther north and with the Ponca in a land called the Keya Paha that is north of the Niobrara River."

"And which group is Two Crows with?" asked Gabe, bringing a questioning frown to Ezra's face. He had not heard about this 'Two Crows' and wondered what that was all about.

Fox answered, "He is on the hunt with his father, *Pa•hin,* in the Keya Paha."

"And how far are we from the place of their hunt?"

"Two, maybe three days," she answered quietly.

And a plan began to form behind the slow growing smile on Gabe's face as he sat back and sipped on his hot coffee. He glanced at Ezra and grinned, gave a slight nod, and stared at the flames.

Ezra sighed heavily, also leaning back then glanced at Fox, "Say, Fox, I've been meanin' to ask you about your people and their beliefs. You said you learned some English from the black robes, but did they also teach you anything about their God?"

"Some, but it was not unlike our beliefs, so I only listened when they taught us about the tongue of the white man."

"So, would you tell me about what your people believe, you know, about what happens after someone dies?"

She squinted at this strange dark-skinned man, then leaned back on the log behind her, tucking her feet under her and began, "We believe in the great Wakanda. Some see him in the sun, some hear him in the thunder, some see him in the strong animals, but he is a wonderful power."

"Is he who your people pray to? You know, when they need something like getting over a sickness or when you have a big problem in your life?" asked Ezra, leaning forward, elbows on his knees and hand holding the steaming coffee.

"Yes. But we do not pray for little things, only things when great power is needed."

"And what about when one dies, what then?" inquired Ezra.

"Everyone has *wanaghe,* or spirit, that goes on after death. We are told by the elders that if we are good, we go to the good ghosts, but if we are bad, we go to the bad ghosts. Four nights after death, the *wanaghe* travels a very dark road, that is why some that remain behind light fires for the four nights to help those that travel the dark road."

"And then what happens," asked Ezra, now sitting forward, interested.

"After those four nights, the *wanaghe* reaches," she pointed to the stars and the milky way, "the trail of stars and travels that road. Then he comes to a place where the road is forked and an old man in a buffalo robe, sits there and points to each one which road to take. One is a short road and when it is followed, they soon come to the place where good ghosts dwell. But the other road never ends and those that follow that road are always crying and never reach the end."

"And what or who decides if the spirit is good or bad?" asked Ezra.

"The old man at the crossroads," answered Fox, a little tenuously, frowning.

"That's the difference between what the Omaha believe, and what we know and believe," stated Ezra, sitting forward to sit his coffee cup down and leaning one elbow on his knee, he reached down with the other and brought up a Bible. "We have learned that wherever we go, the people have different beliefs, so the question is, who it right? They can't all be, and so God, the one true living God who created all things, saw fit to have his words put down in this book so everyone would know the truth." He opened the Bible and held it out to Fox, "You've seen books before, haven't you?"

She glanced at the pages, nodded her head and looked to Ezra, "How do you know you are right, and others are not?"

Ezra grinned, looked down at the pages, and back to Fox, "Because this never changes. The stories your people have of creation, of right and wrong, of walking the trail of stars, just like the stories of all the other people, they change. As they are told from one grandfather to a small child that will one day be a grandfather, the stories change. Not a lot, but a little. And each time a change is made, that shows how wrong it is. Because if it was true, it would never change. That's why God had it written down, so it would not change. Do you understand?"

She paused, thinking, and looked up eyes squinting slightly, "Yes, I have thought that before."

"Good, now here's something very special you need to understand. Getting to Heaven, or as your people have thought of it, taking the trail of stars, is not up to some old man at a crossroads, but is up to you. Not whether we're judged by others to be good or bad, but by a decision we make. That decision is to accept God's plan for us to get to Heaven." Ezra opened the pages of the Bible and began to show and tell Fox about how we are sinners and the penalty for our sin is death and Hell forever, but that God loves us so much He sent His Son to pay the penalty for us so we wouldn't have to. He also gave us the free gift of eternal salvation, but that it is a gift we have to accept.

Fox interrupted Ezra when she asked, "But do we not have to do a lot of good things so we can have that?"

"No, because if we had to earn our way to Heaven, just how much good or how many good things would we have to do? You see, Fox, the Bible tells us in Ephesians chapter two verses eight and nine that it's by grace that we are saved, not of works, or those things we do, and that eternal life is a gift that we have to receive. You see, when it's like that, then the Son of God, Jesus, gets all the credit. When we get to Heaven, we say 'I'm here because of what Jesus did for me, not what I did.'"

"If I receive that gift, will I walk the trail of stars to this Heaven?" asked Fox.

"If you believe in what Jesus did for you with all of your heart, yes you will."

"The old man at the crossroads will not send me the wrong way?"

"Nope."

"Then that is what I want. Will you show me how?"

"Be glad to," answered a grinning Ezra as he began to tell Fox more about Jesus and the free gift of eternal life. He told her how all she had to do was to believe with her whole heart, and ask in prayer for that gift of salvation, and it would be hers. As he quietly led her in prayer, a trail of tears started down her cheek and for the first time in her life she prayed to the eternal God of Heaven and asked to be saved from the penalty of sin and to be given the gift of an eternity in Heaven.

17 / Keya Paha

At the confluence of the Keya Paha and the Niobrara Rivers, Ezra, Gabe and Fox crossed the larger water and pointed the horses due west. With the Keya Paha originating far to the northwest and the Niobrara coming from the southwest, they found themselves in a plain with tall grass waving in the wind and mimicking the rolling waves of the distant ocean. The air was cool and fragrant with the spring flowers casting their scent upon the winds to freshen the land with the smells of spring. The lingering fragrance of the rain contrasted with the leather and horse sweat that rode with the trio.

It was a meditative threesome that crossed the high plains of buffalo country. The migrating herds would leave a broad swath of churned soil and dung in their wake, but so far, they had seen nothing that told of a herd of wooly bison. Fox pointed with her chin to the unspoiled landscape and said, "They have not come yet. My people will be waiting." She lifted her eyes skyward and scanned the terrain, "Soon,

soon they will come. This is the land that draws them," she explained as she waved her arm to take in the wide vista that seemed to stretch interminably.

"It is a big land," acknowledged Gabe, shifting his weight to his stiffened arms that rested upon the pommel. His shoulders were hunched as he stretched his legs and scanned the terrain. Low rolling hills, sparsely covered with a variety of vegetation, stretched away to the north and west. "Those hills look like a herd of turtles, struggling to get to some water or something."

"That is why they are called the Keya Paha, it is Lakota for turtle hills," explained Fox.

"You don't say!" declared Gabe but received a confused frown from Fox.

"I did say," she replied, and added, "Why would I not say?" still frowning at the odd remark.

"Uh, oh, uh, never mind, it's just a saying of my people," stammered Gabe, shaking his head. He heard Ezra chuckle from behind them but refused to give the man the satisfaction of looking at him. Ezra had often said about Gabe that even when he spoke plainly, he could still be hard to understand. He decided to try a different tack to change the subject. "So, if things could be worked out that you could be with Two Crows, you know, to be his woman and stay with your people, would that be alright with you?"

"But I am your woman. You paid my father and I am yours now. I cannot be the woman of two men," she scowled at Gabe, wondering about the thinking of this white man.

Although they had not been together as man and woman, she was still his and could not leave him as that would bring shame on her father. He was the holy man of the Omaha and to shame him was against the way of her people.

"I understand that but do the women of your people ever leave their man and go to another?" asked Gabe.

"No, it is not allowed, unless the man cannot provide for his family, but I have never known that to happen. The man can take another wife, but then there are two women in the lodge, less work for each one," she nodded and smiled as she explained the simple way of living as a family unit with her people.

"But there are some native people, like the Shawnee, that if the woman does not want the man anymore, she just puts his things outside the lodge, and it is done. He must leave, maybe find a different woman and go on from there."

She scowled again, "Go on from where? And to where does he go?"

Again Gabe heard Ezra chuckling behind him, enjoying his frustration and inability to explain something so simple. Gabe continued, "What happens with your people if two people, a man and his woman, no longer want to be together?"

"I know of one time when that happened. The man did not want his woman and took another. The two women fought and the first left in shame because she could not make her man happy."

"And what happened to her, the first wife, I mean?" asked Gabe.

"She left our people and was never seen again. It is said she walked with the ghosts."

"Could she just go with another man instead of leaving?" responded Gabe, his exasperation beginning to show.

"No man would have her; she was shamed."

Gabe twisted uncomfortably in his saddle, looking around. He turned to look back at Ezra and received nothing but a grin and shrugged shoulders from his friend. He shook his head, turned back to look ahead and thought. Suddenly an idea came, "Say, don't your people have some kind of ceremony, celebration, something, when two people are married, or joined?"

Fox smiled and nodded, "Yes. We do, it is very nice. The women all get together and make the dress and more. They give the woman to be joined lots of advice and gifts, she learns how to make her man happy as they talk with her. And the man . . ." but she was interrupted by Gabe's uplifted hand.

"But we didn't have that? Does that mean we are not joined?" he asked.

"My father is the holy man of our village, but we left before there could be a joining ceremony. There is another man with this group of hunters, the war chief," she pointed ahead with her chin, and although she had lost a little of her enthusiasm, she continued, "and he will do that if we want. I have friends there also who will make the dress for me."

He did not respond to her implied suggestion but grew quiet and pensive, thinking about Fox and her life. They rode quietly, the only sounds the creak of the leather and the rattle of stones beneath the horses' hooves, and the occasional blow of a horse. He would do nothing that would hurt her nor shame her, but her being with him was not right. He knew she was a good woman, quite beautiful and a hard worker. She would make someone a good mate, but not him. At best, his future was tenuous, they were bound for the land of many hostile tribes, and with the possible added peril of bounty hunters coming after him as the others had done, it was no life for a man and wife. If only he knew more about the ways and customs of the Omaha people, Gabe knew he would be able to send Fox back with her people to marry Two Crows.

The land was scarred with the tributaries of the rivers both north and south of the travelers with some of the stream beds trickling with spring fed streams, others flowing with runoff from high water tables and overflow from the recent rains. Each scar held deep green foliage from button brush to random cottonwood copses. Ezra spoke into the quiet, "I can see where one day all this could be good farmland," as he stood in his stirrups and waved his arm around. "Those low hills'd make good wind breaks for a home and barn, corrals for the livestock, and even a root cellar. Yessir, this'd make a good farm!" he declared.

Fox reined up and waited for him to come alongside, "What is this farmland?" she asked.

"Well, you know, your people grow beans, squash, corn and such. A farm is just a big garden. A farmer would plow *all* this up, plant crops like wheat for bread, oats for horses, corn for people and livestock, and more."

"They would make all this," motioning to the wide flat prairie land that held tall grass that reached the horses' bellies, "into a place for corn and squash?" she asked, frowning. "Why? One family could not eat all that, even a village like mine could not. That would be a waste."

Ezra looked at the girl, realizing it was now his turn to be a little exasperated in trying to explain the ways of the white man. He shook his head, grinning, "No, it would not just be for his family. What they don't use, they trade to others, like your people do, you know, like when we traded with the Ponca for some of their vegetables."

Fox slowly lifted her head, understanding, and grinned. "Yes, I understand. It is good to trade for what you do not have."

As they traveled, the three stayed within sight of the Niobrara, but always looking to the west for any sign of the camp of the buffalo hunters. It was late afternoon when Gabe, belly down on the highest hillock with the telescope to his eye, gave the word. "There, 'bout three, four miles, might be smoke."

Fox and Ezra were seated cross-legged, holding the leads of the horses as they grazed behind them and both shielded their eyes, leaning forward, trying to spot the camp. Ezra said, "You sure?"

"No, that's why I said, 'might be'," answered Gabe, rolling

to his side to look back at his friend, grinning. He looked to the west, gauged the sun to be close to two hours before setting. "We've got plenty of time, we can probably make that before the sun goes down." He looked to Fox, "There won't be any problem with us ridin' into their camp, will there?"

Fox shook her head, "You have me and the word from Blackbird, the leader of all the Omaha. We will be made welcome."

"The war chief, *Padhin,* is the father of Two Crows, right?" asked Gabe.

Fox's brow furrowed, her eyebrows came low, and she squinted at Gabe as she answered, "Yes."

"And he's the one that does the joining ceremony?"

Fox relaxed, understanding, and lifting her head, answered, "Yes."

"I guess I need to talk to him. Maybe he can explain things for me," resolved Gabe, standing and reaching for the lead on Ebony. Ezra cocked his head to the side, wondering just what was up with his friend. He just hoped it wouldn't get them into more trouble.

18 / Intrigue

Padhin-nanpaji, rested his hands on his knees, his legs crossed before him, as he listened to Gabe tell of the time of his rescue of Running Fox and the subsequent happenings. Little Turtle, the wife of Padhin had seated herself beside and slightly behind her man and listened to the story, often nodding and smiling and giving Gabe the impression she understood exactly where he was going with this story. Gabe he continued. "Now, I don't understand all the ways and customs of your people, but I wasn't ready to take a wife. So, is there any way, maybe your son Two Crows and Running Fox could be together without it causing shame or anything for Fox?"

Little Turtle, smiled, leaned back and waited for her husband to respond. *Padhin,* or He-who-fears-not-the-sight-of-a-Pawnee, sternly looked at the white man and said, "It is not done among our people."

Little Turtle leaned forward and spoke softly to her man,

and the two conferred for a few moments until He-who-fears-not looked to Gabe and said, "Since you have not been joined, there is a way." He looked back at his woman and they spoke some more until she waved him back and he turned again to Gabe. Ezra had sat quietly beside his friend and Fox had gone to another lodge with some friends. The war chief looked from one to another and then spoke to Gabe, "Other white men I have known are not good hunters. You are not a good provider for a woman or a family."

At first, Gabe was insulted, thinking this man knew nothing about him or his ability at hunting or fighting or providing. But it suddenly struck him, and he grinned and answered, "You are right. I am a terrible provider!" He was remembering the simple statement that came from Fox about a man not able to provide for his family that it is allowed for the woman to leave and take another man for her mate.

Ezra began to understand and leaned in, "But, Fox has already seen you provide. You've taken deer on the way and she saw what you did with your bow for the Ponca chief."

Gabe looked at his friend, "No one else has seen that." He looked back to the war chief, "So, if I were to go on the buffalo hunt and miss everything, then what?"

Turtle leaned in and said, "Two Crows would come to her defense, tell everyone you are not a good mate and could not provide for her, but he could." She smiled, folded her arms across her chest and nodded her head to emphasize her point.

"That would be it? Nothing else?" asked Gabe.

"If you wanted to keep her, then you would fight for her. You would be shamed before her people if you did not fight for her," answered the war chief.

"Would she be shamed or hurt in any way?"

Turtle leaned in again, "She would be glad to be free of a man that could not provide for her and the people would think she had done right to refuse to be joined."

"Does Two Crows still want her as his woman?"

Turtle let a slow smile cross her face as she visibly relaxed and looked to her husband. The war chief nodded slowly, "When he left on the hunt, he planned to take many buffalo and show her father he was a good hunter. He planned to go on a raid with the Ponca into the land of the Lakota to steal many horses to give to her father for the price for Running Fox."

Gabe grinned, "That sneaky old man has already gotten the price for Fox. I had to give him a good rifle and more."

Padhin grinned, nodding his head. Turtle chuckled and put her hand to her mouth, "White Elk Woman will be happy to have her back with her people but Black Cloud will try to get more from Two Crows."

"If they are joined before we go back, he can do nothing," answered the war chief, grinning. Both Turtle and the chief knew Black Cloud as the man who always tried to best the other in any trade and he had done so with Gabe. When Black Cloud discovered Fox was no longer with the white man, but joined with Two Crows, he would be considered as bested by the young warrior who gained a woman without paying the father anything.

"But wouldn't that shame Running Fox?"

The two looked at one another, then Turtle said, "My son will give a good price, but later."

Word came that evening of the progress of the migratory herd. The hunt would commence at first light the following morning and Gabe and Ezra would join the Omaha. The war chief had several sub-chiefs that would lead different groups of hunters. Two Crows, as a respected hunter although not a sub-chief, would also lead a group. His band would camouflage themselves with buffalo robes and crawl as close to the herd as possible. Then, armed with bows, they would begin the assault, believing they could silently take several kills before the herd was alarmed.

The sub-chief known as Broken Lance would command the band with rifles. They would be strategically placed, hunkered down in a dry gulch, and would begin shooting only if and when the herd began to move because of the first kills. The third assault would be led by Bear Killer with his band mounted to give chase. These would be armed with lances, bows, and rifles, and since they could pursue their prey, would usually have the greatest number of kills. This group would now include Gabe and Ezra..

As the shadows of early morning stretched across the tall grass, the presence of the herd was told first by the musky smell of thick fur that had rolled in the urine-soaked dirt. Even with rich soil bearing deep grass, a thin cloud of dust hung over the massive brown blanket that moved slowly across the rolling hills and grassy flats. A low rumble, a chorus of grunts, bellows, and shuffling hooves, wafted from around the swinging bearded heads of the wooly beasts that swayed like a great pendulum marking the time till their demise. Black eyes shone from the depths of the matted curls that adorned the ponderous skulls. The beasts, some weighing close to a ton, seemed invincible as they lumbered along at their own pace.

The Ezra and Gabe sat their mounts on the slope of a low bald hill that overlooked the vast prairie. Fifteen other mounted hunters that made up the west group watched the slow approach of the herd. Gabe motioned with his chin, "The other bunch yonder," motioning to the group on the opposite side of the wide plain, "look to be just as anxious as this 'un. I'm hopin' if there's any that are shooting rifles, they make sure they hit them big brown boys and not any of us."

Ezra chuckled and said, "You just remember what you're supposed to be shootin' at, and missing by the way, and we'll be just fine."

The herd numbered in the thousands and was over two hundred yards wide and most of a mile long. Gabe remembered Fox telling of the two larger bands of hunters further south, that would have already taken their kills, perhaps from this same herd. And now these Omaha and Ponca would stock their larders, but even if every hunter were to take two or three buffalo, it didn't seem the herd would be diminished significantly.

"They're doin it!" declared Ezra, nodding toward the first band of bow hunters. The exclamation brought Gabe from his reckoning and he stood in his stirrups to see the first buffalo fall. Although a half-mile from their promontory, the nose-dive of the big beast told of the kill. The camouflaged hunters were hard to make out from this distance, but the dropping of such a massive beast was easily seen. The falling of the first animals did not spook the herd, but the blanket of brown slowly moved away from the action of the hunters.

The big beasts ambled to the west side of the wide valley, heads down, always grazing, but the lead cows watchful. The monstrous bulls behind the herd, smelling blood and death, began to push them onward. Although not sure of the danger, they perceived it as a threat and sought to escape. The herd was restless, but not frightened, until the first rifle shot sounded. The herd jumped as if every animal was connected, as the rattle of rifle fire increased and reverberated across the beasts. Heads came up, bellows sounded, then each one leaned forward, lowered their heads and began to run.

The earth quaked beneath the mounted hunters as Bear Killer shouted his cry to signal the men to start their charge. The excitement exploded within each chest as every man sucked mouths full of air, tinged with dust, and dug their heels into the ribs of their favorite buffalo running horse. This band was coming from the left side and most were armed with rifles or lances, the larger group came from the right side and all were armed with either bows or lances. A mounted hunter using a bow or lance finds it easier to shoot or throw across their body to the left side of the horse. Although some skilled hunters preferred using a lance held low on the right side and driving it into the side of the beast like the knights of old.

The mounted riflemen lay along the necks of their horses, charging after the big woolies. Knowing the first shot would be their best chance for a kill, they waited until they were alongside the beast then carefully chose their shot either behind the ear, of low on the chest behind the front leg. Gabe saw some of the shooters holding their rifles one-handed and putting the muzzle almost in contact with the beast before firing. Others were shooting left-handed, guiding their mounts with their knees and leaning into their shot.

Gabe glanced around, seeing some of the shooters reining off to the side to reload while watching the herd lumber past. Suddenly a big bison stumbled and tumbled end over end just in front of Gabe and Ebony, but the big black stallion lifted his front end and jumped over the big carcass, making Gabe grab at his pommel while gripping the Ferguson rifle all the tighter. They landed without breaking stride and Gabe brought the rifle around, firing it pistol fashion, but making certain the bullet passed under the belly of the nearest bison, doing no harm. He reined Ebony away from the herd and began to reload, catching sight of one of the other hunters watching him, and made as if he was frantically fumbling the reloading. Once the rifle was loaded, Gabe kicked Ebony back into the hunt.

Gabe caught sight of Ezra just as he brought down a nice

cow and reined away to reload. He nodded as he passed and looked for another target. It took all the resolve he could muster to make sure he missed when he shot, but he also made certain someone saw each shot. Finally after three misses, he pulled aside to reload, determined that his mission had been accomplished. He sat on a slight knoll, watching the herd thunder away, still chased by a few resolute hunters. He searched the field of carcasses, looking for Ezra, spotted him as he rode up to a downed carcass and started toward his friend.

They had just started the field dressing, splitting open the beast from tail to tongue, when they heard someone approach. The two friends stood, bloody hands hanging at their side, and watched Running Fox and Little Turtle, together with two other women come close. Fox asked, "Where are your kills?"

Gabe stepped around the carcass and looked at the young woman and answered, "I guess I didn't get any!" shrugging his shoulders and dropping his eyes.

He looked up to see Fox standing agape, surprise registering on her face, "You? You did not kill any buffalo?"

He did his best to appear chastised and regretful, even shamed, "I tried, but I just could not get any," he mumbled as he did his best to appear contrite.

The other women began chattering between one another. Little Turtle turned to Fox, "This is the man you want to feed you and your children? He cannot even take one buffalo!" she waved her arm at the long since disappeared herd. "Even I could take one from so many!"

The other women touched the arm of Fox to get her attention, the buxom one adding, "You should not join with this man! You will starve! Choose from one of the many hunters that have proven themselves." Her remarks elicited similar responses from the other woman and the activity had drawn the attention of others nearby who were coming near to see what was happening. As the others approached, asking questions, several gathered around Fox, consoling and advising her. They were very adamant in their suggestions and animated in their talking.

Suddenly a mounted warrior rode up at a run, sliding to a stop and dropping to the ground even before his mount stopped. He ran to the group, looked to Fox and the women, trying to make sense of the chatter. When his mother explained to him, he turned toward Gabe and shouted, "You are not worthy to be her man! You cannot provide for her lodge! I fight you for her!" Two Crows snatched his tomahawk from his belt and started toward Gabe, prompting the women to shout and draw back. Gabe saw Fox surrounded by the other protective women, then looked to Ezra and said, "Looks like it's time for me to leave. I'll be west of the camp waitin' for you." He nodded toward the carcass, "Make sure you bring some steaks, I've worked up a powerful hunger." He turned and vaulted for Ebony, his foot in one stirrup and swung aboard as the big black leaped away and took off at a full gallop, kicking dirt with his heels that scattered over the criticizing and shouting crowd. Two Crows shook his tomahawk and the retreating white man, shouting, "You are not worthy! She is mine!"

Ezra turned his back to the prattling women and resumed his butchering. As the women and Two Crows started to their own tasks, Ezra sensed someone nearby and turned to see Running Fox, standing alone and looking at him. As he turned to face her, he saw a tear make a furrow in the dusty face as she said, "I know what he did. I am sad, but I am also happy. Tell him I am grateful."

Ezra grinned, nodded his head, and watched as she turned away to follow the woman who had formulated the plan to keep her with the Omaha and with her son, Two Crows. As she started away, Ezra said, "Running Fox, you will be missed." She turned and smiled, and with a simple nod, she walked away.

19 / Lakota

The coffee was hot and steaming as the two friends sat back from the fire to enjoy the moment and savor the treat. The fresh buffalo steaks had been especially tasty, grilled over the flames as they were, and fresh cattail roots roasted in the coals finished the fare. Ezra and Gabe were well satisfied with the meal and now looked at the stars before turning in for the night. The sound of heavy footfalls of two horses told the men they had unexpected visitors. Their rifles near at hand, both men drew the pistols from their belts and lay them across their thighs as they heard from the darkness, "A-ho!"

Gabe answered, "A-ho!" and in the tongue of the Omaha, "Come into the light."

Two Crows and Running Fox had dropped to the ground and led their horses into the ring of light from the campfire. Both Gabe and Ezra stood when they came near and Gabe spoke, "Well, this is a surprise."

Fox stepped forward, smiling, "We want to tell you we are grateful. I told Two Crows that you were a very good hunter and never failed to take down whatever you hunted. His mother, Little Turtle explained what all of you did and we thank you."

Gabe chuckled, and as Ezra offered them both coffee, and began to explain, "Fox, I want you to know that if things were different, I would fight him for you. This is for the best, you two belong together and you wouldn't really want to leave your people."

"I know." She looked to Two Crows, took his hand in hers and back at Gabe, "We have wanted to be together since we were young. We never thought it would be different, and now you have made it possible. Thank you."

They visited a while longer and as the two were ready-ing to leave, Two Crows looked at Gabe, "The Lakota have been a peaceful people, but they are great warriors. Many of the young warriors want to earn honors and will steal, count coup, and kill to do so. If I were to travel through the territory of the Lakota, I would do so at night, and be very watchful."

"That is good counsel, Two Crows. We will do that. What do you know of the tribes beyond the Lakota?" asked Gabe.

"The Arapaho, Cheyenne, and the Shoshoni are all good people. The Cheyenne are friendly, but the Arapaho and the Shoshoni are not so friendly. You travel far, will you be back in the land of the Omaha?"

"Perhaps one day, many summers from now, but for now, we will go west to the mountains, and after that, perhaps beyond."

The men clasped forearms and hands, drew one another close and although Two Crows did not say more, it was evident by his expression that he doubted if the two friends would ever come back, probably thinking they would meet their end somewhere on their travels. Fox hugged both men, said her goodbyes and walked from the light with her man.

Gabe and Ezra looked at one another, and without a word, began packing their gear and readying for their departure. The moon was waxing full and the clear night held the bright stars in place, each one taking its turn to beckon the travelers onward. With the north star off his right shoulder, Gabe led the way. They kept the Niobrara off to the left, staying in the tall grass but with the near shelter of trees and brush along the riverbank if needed.

They had gone but a few miles when the deep shadows before them told Gabe of the many scars of gorges, gullies and ravines that promised difficult going. With a quick scan of the sloping land that stretched toward the river, he chose to cross the Niobrara and hold to the south bank. Two Crows had suggested crossing as soon as possible because the land south of the river was the land of the Brule Lakota, who at present were friendlier than their neighbors to the north.

The rolling hills were dimpled with a few piñon and cedar, an occasional juniper and random sagebrush. The long slope that beckoned them to the river slid slowly to water's edge and the men did not hesitate to ride their horses into the slow-moving stream. The moon gave ample light and the footing proved solid, at least for Ebony and the packhorse that followed.

But Ezra and his bay chose their own route just a little downstream, and within moments the pack horse was fighting his lead and jerked Ezra into the water. The splashing and shouting split the quiet of the night and Gabe kicked Ebony out of the water onto a gravel bar, snatched his rawhide riata from the saddle and uncoiled a loop to lay in the water within reach of Ezra. Gabe leaned against the taut rope and pulled Ezra to the sandbar. He looked up to see the packhorse struggling and Ezra sputtered, "Quicksand!" Gabe looked again and turned back to Ebony, stepping quickly aboard and rolling another loop. He rode Ebony deeper into the water, cautious with every step, and when within about fifteen feet, he swung the loop over his head and threw it. The big loop dropped over the thrashing head of the horse, and Gabe pulled it taut, took a wrap around the horn and turned Ebony back toward the far bank. The big black responded to Gabe's urging and leaned into the riata, pulling it taut and the neck of the pack horse stretched out. The chestnut rocked back and forth, finally freeing his front legs and pawed at the water, his head dipping beneath the current as he stumbled, but lifted again. Ebony dug for more leverage and within seconds, the chestnut was free and splashing up behind the big black.

Ezra was stretched out on the gravel shoal, catching his

breath, and sat up to see the big black carry Gabe up the far bank. The bay stood beside his master, looking down as if to ask what he was doing laying on the ground, and Ezra said, "Alright, alright," and stood to mount. Gabe had dropped the riata that hung around the pack horse's neck beside Ezra and he now picked it and the lead rope up and started up the bank after Gabe.

"What some people won't do just to get a dip in the river!" chided Gabe as Ezra came near.

"You should talk, it wouldn't hurt you to take a bath once in a while!" declared Ezra.

"You wanna ride, what with your britches drippin'?" kidded Gabe.

"You just lead on, I'll be right behind you!" declared an obstinate Ezra.

They stayed within sight of the river but kept to the flats for easy traveling. The shuffling
gait of the horses prompted them to look for a site to stop and give the horses a breather, maybe a little graze and water. A cluster of cottonwood at the edge of a shallow creek bed beckoned and they stopped and stepped down, loosening the girths and leading the horses to a shallow pool of fresh water that came from a thin trickle of spring water. Gabe paused, lifting his head and sniffing, "You smell that? I think it's woodsmoke. Somebody's camped nearby."

Ezra's nostrils flared as he sniffed the air, nodded his head and answered, "It's purty weak, might just be another traveler."

"But it could be a camp that's a bit further away."

"Reckon," answered Ezra.

Gabe motioned with his head as he slipped his Ferguson from the scabbard, "I'm gonna climb that little rise yonder and see if I can locate it." He checked the loads in the rifle and his belt pistol, and satisfied, started for the knoll.

It was just a short while until he returned and reported, "I think it's a village, probably Lakota. Two Crows said they would be in this area, and that camp is on the bank of the Niobrara. I think it might be best if we swing further south and around them. If we go wide enough we should be alright."

"How big is the village?" asked Ezra.

"Can't rightly say, but it's big. With it bein' so late an' all, not many cookfires. But my guess would be about a hundred lodges. That big moon showed those tipis pretty clear."

As they swung south and away from the Niobrara, the terrain changed dramatically. The flat lands had become an endless stretch of hills, all looking like biscuits in a big pan and rising as obstacles on their trail. It was either stay in the cuts between the hills and follow the twists and turns of the draws or ride the tops of the hills with the continual up and down as they worked through the short grass and scrub sage. After quickly tiring of thick brush in the bottoms, they took to the hilltops and the rise and fall of the trail. Occasionally coming to a bit of flat grassland, they walked beside the horses, letting them crop an occasional mouthful as they moved.

When they came to a cluster of juniper with an out-of-place ponderosa in the midst, Gabe chose to make camp before the sun caught them on the trail. The trees hugged the bottom edge of a slope that had been carved by a trickle of a stream and offered its waters to the thirsty travelers. A quick little fire under the outstretched limbs of the largest juniper and coffee was ready. They finished off the last of the flame broiled buffalo steak and soon stretched out on their blankets. The horses were tethered nearby, within reach of both grass and water, and the snores of Ezra kept any prowling night creatures at bay. Gabe chuckled as he struggled to find sleep, but he soon joined Ezra in slumber.

Something tugged at Gabe's consciousness, trying to bring him awake. He smelled meat cooking but heard nothing. He forced his eyes open, the dark shade of the juniper staying the bright sun from his face, and slowly looked about. The horses stood hip-shot, sleeping in the shade of the ponderosa and another juniper. Even Ebony, the first to give a warning of any danger, showed heavy eyelids and a slow swishing tail ridding him of an aggravating fly. Gabe slowly moved his head to the side, expecting to see Ezra by the fire, but was startled to see a native, long grey hair dangling loosely over his shoulders and reaching to the top of his breech cloth, the only item of clothing he wore save the moccasins. A knife rested in a scabbard at his belt and a tomahawk hung loosely at his other hip. He sat on the log, elbows resting on his knees, hands clasped together, as he looked unflinching at Gabe. A quick glance showed Ezra was still snoring, only not as loudly, but sound asleep.

Gabe looked at the old man, furrowed his brow and pushed the blankets down as he sat up. The old man watched, unmoving, with a slow grin cutting his face. Gabe stood, flipped his belt around his waist and slipped the hawk in at his hip, put the belt pistol behind the buckle, and with a glance at the old man, walked to the trees for his morning constitutional. When he returned, the old man had not moved and Gabe, using sign, asked, "Who are you, why are you here?"

"I am Big Thunder, and I am hungry."

20 / Thunder

Ezra had kept some choice cuts, the loin, hump, haunch and more of the buffalo cow he had taken, and several strips cut by Big Thunder were broiling over the flames of the cook-fire. Yampa roots were baking in the coals, and hot water chugged on a flat rock beside the fire. Big Thunder had little knowledge of the white man's coffee, but he knew they started with hot water. He quietly watched the two men rolling up their bedrolls and sorting their packs as they waited for the food to be ready.

Ezra saw the pot begin to dance and he put in a handful of coffee grounds, shook it around a little, then set it back on the rock to finish brewing. He looked up at the old man and asked in sign, "Are you Lakota?"

"Yes, I am *Sičháŋǧu* or some whites call us Brule," with the tribal name in sign being the 'Burnt Thighs Nation.'

"Why are you here alone?" asked Ezra, sitting down on the nearest cottonwood trunk.

"We talk after we eat," signed the old man, reaching for one of the willow branches that held a strip of steak.

As they sat back, Ezra offered the old man a cup of coffee which he gladly accepted, and Gabe said, "Alright, we've eaten. Now, why are you here and alone?" During the meal, the three had discovered the old man was conversant in the language used by the Omaha, Osage and others. With little difficulty, and the combination of words and signs they spoke easily.

"To guide you," nodding to Ezra, "to the village of the Maroons," explained Big Thunder.

Ezra and Gabe frowned at one another, then to the old man as Ezra asked, "Guide me? To the Maroons? I don't understand."

The old man squirmed a little on his seat and said, "Are you not of the Maroons?"

Before Ezra could respond, Gabe asked, "Are you saying there is a village of Maroons nearby?"

Ezra stuttered, looking from his friend to their visitor, and asked Gabe, "Are you talking about the Maroons from the deep south?"

The old man spoke a little tentatively as he started to explain, "All of those like you," nodding toward Ezra, "are of that village. Are you not?"

Ezra looked askance to his friend, "I've never heard of any Maroons except those they called the Black Seminole and some down by New Orleans."

"Most of those I studied about were in Jamaica. But there were those with the Seminole and others, but I've never heard of any this far north. All of those were escaped slaves that banded together and lived in the swamps and such, but now he's saying there's some here. That'd be a first," suggested Gabe.

Ezra leaned forward, holding his coffee with both hands as he leaned on his knees. He looked to the old man, "Tell me about this village. How long has it been there?"

The grey-haired one sighed heavily and began, "They came after the time of greening, last summer. There were many in our village that had been taken with the spotted disease," he pointed at several round scars, typical of small-pox, on his chest and neck, "and helped our people. When it passed, many of our women that lost their mates, went with the Maroons. I was asked to guide them to a place to make a village and to help them. My woman and son were taken by the fever and I agreed to be their guide. There were others like you," nodding to Ezra, "that I have guided to the village to be with the Maroons."

"So, how many are there in this village?" asked Gabe.

The old man looked skeptically at Gabe but answered by holding up all fingers of both hands and flashing them three times, but added, "Perhaps more."

Ezra asked, "You said there were some women of your people that went with them, are there others?"

He nodded his head, grinning, "There are Chickasaw, Choctaw, Tunica and Quapaw, also."

"Are all the women native?" asked Gabe.

"No, there are women, like him," nodding again toward Ezra, "and there are native men also."

Ezra thought a moment, "Have you taken a woman among the Maroons?"

The old man slowly grinned, and nodded, smiling.

"Is the village far?" asked Gabe.

Big Thunder looked at the white man, "There are no white men in the village."

"Is the village far?" he asked again.

"Two days," and he nodded to the northwest.

Gabe looked at Ezra, "You want to have a look-see at this village?"

"Yeah, I would," he chuckled, "I'm interested."

They still chose to travel at night, making room on the chestnut pack horse for Big Thunder, who was quite happy to be riding for a change. The first night was a peaceful ride as the moon was close to full and the sky was clear, dotted only by the myriad of heavenly lanterns that continually beckoned them onward. As the second night began, they moved away from the north bank of the Niobrara and took a due west, sometimes northwest, route. Just as first light turned the black of night to dim grey, Big Thunder bid them stop at the edge of a bluff that overlooked a thick forest of towering ponderosa dropping away into a land of peaks and scars that showed as claw marks of the Creator as he carved out the ravines and valleys below, made all the more foreboding by the deep shadows of early morning.

The men looked at the beginning colors of sunrise and to the land before them. The drastic contrast in terrain was startling to the travelers that had ridden the endless rolling hills and limitless grasslands for what seemed like eons of time. The stark land stretched to the northeast and away to the west beyond the limits of their eyesight. It seemed to rise up before them and dare them to enter, skeletal fingers of bony ridges captured their attention and mocked their hesitation. Gabe turned to Big Thunder, and with a scowl that spoke of skepticism, asked, "The village is down there?"

Thunder pointed to a long slow, almost barren slope that appeared as the source of the tree lined scars and ended at a confluence of gullies. "It is beyond that point."

Gabe guessed the landmark to be about two miles distant, "And is it far from that point?"

"Not far. They know we come."

Gabe gave the old man a quick glance, surprised at his statement, "They know? How?"

"We have been watched and a scout has been sent," he pointed to a thin trail of dust that contrasted with the deep green of the pine.

They followed the grassy finger flat to the point and dropped off the flat-top into a beautiful green valley. Gabe thought it resembled the palm of a hand with each of the fingers being an aspen and pine filled ravine that reached back to the top of the buttes. Nestled in the palm of the valley was an unusual assortment of hide tipis, earthen lodges, and brush arbor huts. A serene scene of familiarity greeted the small party of visitors. Cookfires held pots and delightful smelling preparations, several women were busy at the fires while others tended drying racks or scraped hides. Children with minimal clothing ran after one another, some chasing a hoop with a stick, while others had small bows and blunted arrows. There were numerous horses, some tethered near the lodges, but most were grazing together on a wide meadow near the valley bottom stream. Gabe had to stop to take it all in, surprised they had not been greeted by a party of warriors as had happened in other villages. He smiled at the picture of tranquility, unexpected in this wild land.

Big Thunder led them to an earthen lodge that sat somewhat by itself at the edge of the encampment with a family group sitting near the cookfire. A tall black man stood as they neared, hands hanging at the sides of his beaded buckskins. He wore moccasins, buckskin britches, a long fringed and beaded tunic, all of which fit him well and showed his broad shoulders and muscled chest, arms and legs. A mixture of confidence and curiosity flashed from his dark eyes, but a grin tugged at the corners of his mouth as Big Thunder stepped down from the chestnut. He was warmly greeted by the man he introduced as Jean Saint Malo.

Gabe frowned and asked, "I read of a Jean Saint Malo that was a leader of the Maroons in Spanish Louisiana, but he was executed ten, fifteen years past. Is that right?"

The big black man crossed his arms over his chest and answered, "That was my father. Before he was captured, he directed me to take these people as far from New Orleans as possible. He said only distance could give us freedom." He looked from Gabe to Ezra, "You are both welcome to our village. I take it Thunder has explained to you about our people?"

As both men stepped down, Ezra answered, "He has told us some, but I, or rather we, are very curious to know more."

"We will eat, and I will tell you all you want to know," suggested Jean, nodding to Thunder to take the horses away. "Thunder will take your things to a camp nearby. We have no lodges to spare or we would give you one, but you are welcome to camp there, at the tree line. It is a good place for you and your animals."

A stately and very attractive woman came from the lodge, hands full of things for the meal, and nodded at the men as she passed. Jean saw Ezra look at the woman with a slight frown and he said, "She is my wife, Stands Tall, she is from the Osage people."

Ezra and Gabe looked at one another, smiling, and Gabe turned back to Jean, "We spent last winter with the Osage. They are good people."

Ezra explained, "That is why your woman caught my eye. It is not often you see a native woman so tall, except among the Osage."

"Our village has people from many lands and bands," answered Jean, motioning the men to be seated and continued, "If you know of the Maroons, you know that many were slaves, but not all. When my father led our people, we lived in the swamps and controlled the waterways from Lake Borgne and Lake Pontchartrain to the Gulf. Some of us hid and others fled when the Spanish militia came. When my father was taken, we had prepared to leave and moving only at night, we followed the mighty river to the north. Some joined the Choctaw, Chickasaw and others, and some took wives from among these people and came with us. My father told of the many bands on the islands and some of those came to our lands and joined with us."

"Have you found the freedom you sought?" asked Ezra, leaning forward in interest.

"Yes, but it has been hard, but it is the same for our people wherever we are, do you not find it so?"

"Not the same as you and your people. I was freeborn, and my father is the pastor of a large church in Philadelphia, but there have been times my freedom has been threatened," answered Ezra, noticing Gabe sit back and listen as these men talked about things only they could truly understand.

Gabe watched and listened and at a lull, he asked, "Have you been accepted by the natives? I mean, there are many different tribes and not all are at peace with one another. Have you found any to be openly hostile to you?"

"Probably not much different than what the two of you would encounter," answered Jean, "Most are understandably cautious, but we have helped some, like the Lakota, and received help from some. We do our best to earn the trust of our neighbors." He motioned around, "Feel free to move about our village and speak with our people. You will find those from many different groups among us. The one thing we have in common is that both natives and negroes have been subjected to slavery and will join together to fight against that."

Ezra chuckled, "We," motioning to himself and Gabe, "both understand that all too well." He went on to tell Jean of their encounter with the French voyageurs turned slave traders and of their freeing the Pawnee captives. "So, even though the Spanish have outlawed slavery, at least for the natives, it didn't stop the French!"

"Yes, but the Spanish still keep slaves. That is why they were so against my father and the Maroons. The man that took my father, Colonel Francisco Bouligny, swore to hunt down every Maroon that escaped, no matter how long it took nor how far he had to go. He has risen even higher in power and has the entire Spanish force at his whim. Word has come that he has sent letters to Santa Fe for additional Soldado de cuera to aid in his search for Maroons."

"Well, I think he would have a mighty difficult time finding you this far from New Orleans," suggested Ezra.

"We are free, not because we assume we are safe, but because we never rest. We grow in numbers, but even with all our people, the Spanish could bring a force that would be two or three times greater, and all would be fighting men." He looked up to see his wife motioning and turned back to his guests, "Enough of this talk. Let us eat and enjoy each day that our God gives to us!"

21 / Soldados

The two officers, Capitan Andrés de Cerranza and Lieutenant Alvar Nuñez Cabesa de Vaca, leaned over the weathered map, the Capitan pointing as he spoke, "The trader, Juan Munier, has his post here at the mouth of the Niobrara. According to his last message, the Two Kettle Sioux have told of a village of blacks, he called them Maroons, somewhere around here," pointing to the map, "north of the Niobrara and due north of the confluence of the North and South Platte Rivers."

"How reliable is that information?" asked the Lieutenant. Nearby stood Sergeant Abelardo Valazquez, watching over the shoulder of the Lieutenant. Besides the difference in rank, a greater division was always present between the officers and the lower ranks because the officers were always chosen from the Criollo, or pure Spaniard blood people, while the others were recruited from the Mestizo, or mixed bloods that had a combination of Spanish, Indian, and Negro blood, and some were Hispanicized Indians. These had been recruited from the Comancheria and Genizares areas and often included both slaves and free Negroes. The Sergeant had proven himself in battle with the French, the Maroons, and Indians on several occasions and had recently received his promotion. Still uncomfortable with being around the officers, he paid close attention to everything they did and said, eager to gain any advantage or promotion possible. As a sergeant, he was paid 350 pesos a year, more than he could make at any other job that could be had for a Mestizo.

"These are the maps from the Villasur expedition, are they not?" asked Lieutenant de Vaca.

"They are, but they are the best available and have proven to be quite good." The Capitan prided himself in his perfect Castilian tongue, but often lapsed into the language of the common man to make himself understood by others. He was a man of noble birth and had chosen to serve with the *Dragones de Cuera,* and with his family's connections with the governor of Santa Fe de Nuevo México, he hoped for rapid promotion to *teniente coronel graduado,* or Lieutenant Colonel by brevet. Then he could propose marriage to his sweetheart, Maria Del Castillo, the daughter of the Viceroy of Nuvea Vizcaya.

"We have already been on the trail for three weeks, and it has been a hard trail. How much longer will it take? The men and horses are tired and could use some rest," complained the Lieutenant. Sergeant Velazquez had spoken with the officer that afternoon on the trail and he knew the words were his as the junior officer addressed his superior.

The Capitan stood tall and straight, always neat and tidy and proper in his uniform even on the dusty trails they had traveled. He scowled at the Lieutenant and snarled, "You think I do not know that?" He glared at the junior officer and continued, "It is about two days to the junction of these rivers," he jammed his finger on the map, "and we will rest. We will send out scouts to find the village of the Maroons before we move from that spot! There will be plenty of time to rest and to take game for the men."

"Si, Capitan. You are right, Capitan. It is good, Capitan," groveled the junior officer, glancing with a scowl at the Sergeant, who dropped his gaze and remained silent.

With a wave of his hand the Capitan dismissed the two men, sending them scurrying away from the officer's tent toward the scattered garrison. The company totaled forty-one men. Two officers, the sergeant and two corporals, and thirty-six privates, who included a drummer, and armorer, and three carabineers, or sharpshooters. A lone scout, a freed negro slave, had also repeatedly proven himself on other expeditions and was the only man that had been to the region of the Platte Rivers. Each man of the garrison was armed with a musket, a pair of pistols, a bow and arrows, a sword, a lance and a bull-hide shield. They wore a cuera, or multi-layered deer-skin leather jacket without sleeves that protected them from most arrows and gave them the name of Soldado de cuera. They also had chaps attached to the pommel of their saddle to protect the legs and thighs. They were all excellent horsemen, and most had been proven in battle. Now their

mission was to capture the remaining Maroons that had escaped from the New Orleans sweep intended to take them all
and export them to Sierra Leone.

Always the one for the chain of command, the sergeant
passed the word to Corporal Lorenzo Dominguez and Corporal Pasqual Iglesias, who in turn told the rest of the men of
the plan for the next two days and the promise of rest when
they reached the Platte. One of the men grumbled, "But when
we get there, the orders will change! There won't be any rest!"

Others mumbled their agreement until Corporal Dominguez answered, "If nothing else, the horses will probably lay
down and not go any further without rest and graze. We
don't have to worry!"

"So, you're sayin' the horses have more sense than the
officers?" asked another.

"That's why they call it 'horse sense!'" replied the grinning
Corporal Iglesias, the favorite of the men.

"But what are we gonna do about them out there?" asked
another, nodding his head to the darkness.

"What do you mean, Private?" asked Corporal Dominguez.

"Them Indians, I think the scout, Estavanico, said they
were Arapaho."

They had been in Arapaho country for three days and
the Indians had made no secret of their presence with small
bands always following the soldiers at a distance, usually to
the side of their long garrison, but letting themselves be seen.

"The Sergeant didn't say anything about any Indians,

other than those with the Maroons, but I'm sure we have nothing to be concerned about. None of those savages are dumb enough to attack a force the size of ours," reassured the Corporal.

"Unless they can muster a bigger bunch!" mumbled one of the men, as he tossed out the dregs of his coffee. "If they're anything like the Comanche, they'll wait till they get enough so they outnumber us three or more to one, then they'll hit us. All they see are the horses and the guns and such. They don't care the first thing about killin' all of us." He was one of the four former slaves and had been on a number of campaigns. He was one of the most respected fighters and the others looked up to him. He was known as Daniel Wheeler and even though he wore no insignia of office, the others often followed his lead. He turned away to go to his blankets, prompting others to follow suit.

The six coloreds, and the scout whenever he was in camp, kept to themselves and since just a week back when they found out about their mission, they had often talked into the night about what they would do when they came face to face with other former slaves and freed men. The most vocal of the group, Daniel Wheeler, had been the one to ask the questions about the Arapaho. Now he lay on his blankets, hands behind his head and staring at the stars, when another man, Jedidiah Green, asked, "Do you really think you can shoot another colored?"

"Anybody that shoots at me, I don't care what color he is, red, brown, black or white, I'm gonna shoot him first!" declared Daniel in a strong whisper.

"What about hangin' 'em?" asked Ezekiel Carpenter. "I

heard the Capitan sayin' he weren't takin' none of 'em back to Nahl'ns. He'd hang any of 'em that weren't kilt!"

"Ain't gonna have no part in no hangin'! No man should hang, ain't right! When they hang 'em cuz o' the color o' their skin . . . uhn uhn, no sir, ain't gonna be no hangin'!" declared Daniel, shaking his head in the dark. He had seen his own father whipped and hung because the overseer said he was sassin' him, which he never did a day in his life, but they hung him anyway. That was the day Daniel ran away and it was a sight he swore he would never see again.

"Bet we could join 'em," suggested Jedidiah, voicing the thought that had flitted in and out of each of the men's minds since they found out about their orders.

"Now, how you gonna do that? I can just see this whole garrison surroundin' their village and you jumpin' off yore horse and shoutin' 'Wait, wait, I wanna join 'em 'fore you kills 'em!'"

The others chuckled into the darkness but understanding what Ezekiel meant. Even if they wanted to join the Maroons, how could they?

"I been thinkin' on that," mumbled Daniel.

"And?" asked Ezekiel.

"I tell you when I'm done thinkin'!"

"Shhhhh, the Corporal's comin'!" warned another.

They drew their blankets up against the cool night and snuggled down to at least pretend to sleep, anything to avoid the wrath of their leaders. As they did, they were also pondering what they could possibly do to be as free as those they sought. The freedom, if it could be called that, they now had as soldiers was better than slavery, but not much. They still had those that lorded over them, taunting them with their superiority and position, and if they didn't toe the line, they were punished nearly as severely as when they were slaves. All bore the scars of the whip on their backs and harbored the deep resentment against those that had enslaved them and thought of them as little more than animals.

Daniel had been a field worker and a house slave, and his mother had taught him about the times of the Bible and about slaves in those times. He had taught himself to read and devoured many books in the Massa's library and had read of slavery in every time and on every continent. He had known of slaves of almost every race, Oriental, Indian, colored, Mestizo, and even some light skinned mulattos that could have passed for white. He had known of the Maroons since his time in the swamps of Louisiana as an escapee, but he never found their camp. Instead, he had made it to El Paso where he was conscripted into the Soldados. He often thought he had just escaped one type of slavery only to be taken into another.

One thing he knew, and that was where they were going there were no Presidios with Soldados, and it was a vast land. Maybe he could join up with the Maroons, but would that way of life be any better? At least now he was paid. It was only 290 pesos a year, but he did have money which he never had before. Even privates could get promotions, and some had been known to get land grants. As a Maroon, there would be freedom, but what would be the price?

22 / Maroons

Gabe wasn't as disciplined about it as was Ezra, but he was learning and now he enjoyed his morning time with the Lord as he sat at the foot of an isolated ponderosa that was crowded about by juniper and oak brush. He sat facing east, watching the beginning of light sprinkle the light grey dust across the thin line of the eastern horizon. Ezra had left the camp before him and Gabe knew he was within shouting distance, if need be, probably seated much like himself, facing east and watching the dawn arrive. Although many natives were compelled by their beliefs to make offerings and their prayers to the rising sun, Gabe just liked to watch the beginning of the new day and to start it with a heartfelt conversation with his God.

The smell of smoke coming from the direction of their camp alarmed him and he rose to return. As he stepped from the trees, he was surprised to see an Indian woman busy at the fire, cooking a meal. She looked up and seeing Gabe, she smiled, "JeanSaintMalo," pronouncing his complete name as one word, "sent me to cook for you." She spoke in the Siouan tongue, common to the Omaha, Ponca and Osage, although differing somewhat from the Lakota.

Gabe grinned, "That was not needed, but we are grateful."

"It is an honor. He said you are a friend to the Maroon and to the native people. I am from the Two Kettle Lakota. The Maroons helped our people and after I lost my man to the spotted disease, I chose to come with them."

"Have you taken a man from among the Maroon?" asked Gabe, making conversation while he prepared the coffee. He sat the pot of water by the flames and seated himself on the cottonwood log, looking up to the woman for her answer.

"No, I have not."

"I see, oh, my name is Gabe and my friend, is Ezra," remarked Gabe as he saw Ezra returning to the camp from his time on the hillside.

"I am Beaver Woman. Your food will be ready soon," she explained, stirring something in the shallow skillet. Gabe frowned, leaning over to look in the skillet and asked, "What is that?" Ezra seated himself nearby, watching without speaking, but grinning at his friend.

She smiled, answering, "That is timpsila. This is the time of year when they are plentiful. I dug the root and ground it into meal after it was dried." She added several thin sliced strips of the remaining buffalo and stirred the concoction together. Gabe thought it looked like sliced potatoes and smiled as he leaned back, having his attention distracted by the coffee pot beginning its dance on the flat rock. He scooped up a handful of fresh ground coffee that he had been grinding on the flat rock, replaced the lid and nodding toward the pan, "That smells good and I'm getting hungry."

Beaver smiled and reached for the plates, offering one to each of the men. She dished up a plate full and the men poured their own coffee. Beaver sat back to watch the men, ready to offer more if needed. Both enjoyed the morning fare, but before they could refill their plates, their attention turned to a small group approaching their camp. Both men stood, looking at the visitors, four men, three colored and one native, walking forward with purpose, obviously angry.

One lean black man, bare-chested and wearing only rough linen britches was about the same size as Gabe, broad shouldered and with a chest and arms that showed a lot of hard work in the field, stepped forward, holding a flintlock rifle across his chest, eyes flaring. He snarled, "You!" pushing his rifle forward away from his chest but not pointing it directly at either man, "You leave! Now!" he ordered. The three other men stepped to the side, each man armed, one with a rifle, one with a pistol and the native with a lance.

Gabe showed no alarm, but answered in a calm voice, "Your leader, Jean, said we are welcome and could stay as long as we want."

The man with the pistol thrust it into his belt and stepped forward, grabbing Beaver and jerking her away from the fire. She fought him, but the big man muscled her back to their group. Ezra stepped forward, but the leader of the group brought his rifle to bear, cocking the hammer as he leveled it at Ezra, stopping him.

"He had no right to tell you to stay! I am James Parkinson and I should be the leader and I tell you to go! We have sworn to kill anyone that threatened our people and every white man is a threat! You leave or we will kill you!" growled the leader.

"Does that go for my friend here?" asked Gabe, nodding toward Ezra. He was measuring the mettle of the men before him. He knew he had his belt pistol and the hawk in his belt as well as the knives at his back. His rifle lay by the log, but out of reach. He was trying to remember if he saw Ezra's pistol at his belt but wasn't certain.

"Any man that is a friend of our enemy is our enemy!" spat Parkinson. The others grunted and nodded, their stance and glare showing they were anxious to attack.

Gabe looked from one to another, slowly nodding his head. He recognized Parkinson as a man that was used to forcing his way on others and one that was anxious to prove himself in front of his followers. Gabe said, "Alright. We'll just pack up our stuff and leave."

"No!" shouted Parkinson, prodding Gabe with the muzzle of the rifle, "You will leave with what you have! The rest stays!" He jammed the muzzle against Gabe's chest, pushing him backwards, "That's the price you pay for your life!"

Gabe stepped back, eyes wide, feigning fright, and lifting his hands to his side, "Alright, alright! I don't wanna die! Careful with that thing," he slowly stepped back, glancing toward Ezra. He looked down at Ezra's waist, the glance catching Ezra's attention.

As Gabe expected, Parkinson pushed his advantage and followed Gabe as he backpedaled. When the man thrust his rifle forward to strike Gabe's chest again, Gabe slapped it aside drawing his pistol and cocking it in one motion. He brought the pistol muzzle up under Parkinson's chin and growled, "That's not very neighborly of you. Now," he looked from one to the other of the remaining three, none appearing as if they ever had a thought of their own, and now stood under the barrel of Ezra's pistol which he had drawn as the other watched their leader. At Ezra's command, they had dropped their weapons.

"Let me explain to you what it means to be neighborly," growled Gabe. He jammed the muzzle of his pistol hard under the man's chin, snatching his knife from his scabbard as he did, tossing it aside. "You see, my father always taught me to be neighborly, or what he called hospitable. He would say, 'Gabe, my boy, you should always be friendly with folks unless they show themselves unfriendly. Then you might have to explain, in their own terms, just what it means to be friendly.'" He laid the pistol on the grey log along with his hawk and knives and turned back to the angry man.

"He said, 'Sometimes they have to feel it right here!'" and Gabe brought his fist from his side and buried it in Parkinson's gut, bending him over as Parkinson grunted and grabbed his middle. "And sometimes it's a thinkin' matter!" As the man started to straighten up, Gabe chopped down on his head with both hands clasped together, dropping Parkinson to his face in the dirt.

"But then he would say, 'That's the hardest thing for them to do is to learn to think friendly,'" Gabe was talking as he stepped to the side of Parkinson who had drawn himself up on his hands and knees, looking for his hospitality teacher. Gabe said, "My pa quite often had to just beat it into me," he grunted as he brought his fist up from the ground to smash into Parkinson's face, knocking him to his back. The big man, now frantically trying to get to his feet, lunged up and charged Gabe, arms wide, growling through the blood that came from his split lips and busted teeth. One eye was puffy and swollen and would soon be shut, but fire flared from behind the dark lids and scowled visage, but he grabbed only air as Gabe stepped aside, bringing his right fist hard into the man's kidney.

The enraged leader of the small group spun around, one hand on his side, feeling the pain of the kidney punch, and breathing deeply he dropped into a crouch, "I'm gonna kill you white man, but first I'm gonna tear your arms off and smash your face in," but his braggadocio was stopped by a staccato of left jabs that beat his swollen eye and broke his nose as he staggered back on his heels.

"You were saying?" asked Gabe as he dropped his hands to his side and stepped in front of the man, weaving side to side, watching his one eye. Parkinson surprised him as he brought a left roundhouse that caught Gabe beside his ear, knocking him sideways and making him stumble over the stack of firewood. The wood scattered in a clatter and Gabe kicked at it, trying to catch his balance but falling on his back, knocking the air from his lungs. Then the big man landed squarely on top, grabbing Gabe's outstretched arms in an iron grip. The bare-chested beast growled and said, "Now!" Parkinson coughed up a gob of phlegm and spat in Gabe's face. He then started to bring his forehead down to smash Gabe's nose, but the blonde squirmed and arched his back, throwing the bigger man off and with a quick twist, he freed himself and squirmed out and away.

Gabe jumped to his feet and turned just in time to meet the charge of the big man and with a slight twist he caught the man's swing as a glancing blow on his cheek, but rallied as he bent his widespread knees and brought his fist from the ground and buried it in the black man's belly. He brought it back and did it again, and when Parkinson leaned over his fist, Gabe chopped a left into his right ear. As he fell, Gabe brought up his knee, smashing it into his rib cage so hard he heard a bone break; then he let Parkinson fall to the ground.

Parkinson grunted and groaned, pushed himself up and with considerable effort came to his feet. Somehow he had gotten a knife, and now held it low, blade up as he bent into a crouch, scowling with his one eye, snarling with his bleeding lips painting his teeth red. He spit blood and more as he slowly came toward Gabe. Taking a similar stance, arms wide, Gabe matched the man step for step, and when Parkinson feinted, Gabe sucked in his abdomen and stretched to tip toes, the blade barely missing his gut, but Parkinson brought it back and snagged Gabe's tunic, laying it open and drawing blood in a thin streak across his stomach muscles.

The tall blonde stepped back, and watched his attacker's eyes, then as they flared and he lunged forward, Gabe stepped to the side, dropping his open hand on Parkinson's wrist and brought up his right hand to also grab the same wrist in a tight grip, thumbs extended to the back of the man's hand. As Parkinson lifted his arm, Gabe let it come up, stretched it high and with all his force brought it straight down, thumbs at the back of his hand and wrist held in an iron grip. When the knife hand came almost to the waist, both men heard the crack as the arm broke just behind the wrist. Gabe released his grip and stepped back as Parkinson screamed and grabbed his arm, dropping to his knees.

One of Parkinson's friends jumped for his rifle as the Indian, having grabbed his lance, lunged forward seeking to impale Ezra. Ezra snapped off a shot with his pistol, taking the black man with the shot just under his arm high on his chest and with a quick side-step, smashed the pistol barrel across the nose of the Indian as the lance tore at the edge of his tunic at his side. The second Maroon scrambled for his pistol, but Ezra twisted the barrels of his own, bringing the second charged barrel and flash-pan around as he cocked the hammer. When the Maroon came up with his pistol he laughed, and cocked his weapon, thinking he had but one shot, but as Ezra's pistol barked and spat smoke and lead, the man's eyes flared in fear and shock and he started to shout but the ball of lead smashed his teeth into his mouth before it tore a hole in the back of his neck. The would-be assailant died without being able to speak another word, choking on his own blood.

Gabe snatched up his pistol, looked around and seeing no further threat, slipped it behind his belt. He flexed his fingers, wincing a little, but a commotion from the camp caught his attention. The gunshots had brought several running, thinking they were under attack but when they came near and saw the men on the ground, one dead, another shot and one with a mangled face, as well as Parkinson, still on his knees holding his arm and shaking his head in pain, they stopped. The crowd slowly came closer, but a shout from behind stopped them and they parted to let Jean Saint Malo come to the fore. He looked at the men on the ground, looked to Ezra and Gabe, "What happened?"

"Mr. Parkinson wanted us to leave and to leave without our things. I didn't think that was neighborly, so I explained to him what it was to be hospitable," motioning to the man still on his knees. He noted no one had gone to the side of any of their attackers. Gabe looked back at Saint Malo, "Was this your idea?"

"No. Parkinson's brother was Leonard Parkinson, one of the early leaders of the Maroons and a respected man among us. James there," nodding toward the man, "thought he should be a leader because his brother was, and there were some that followed him," motioning to the others on the ground. "This trouble has been brewing for some time. However, we have a rule that if anyone takes the life of another among us, he must leave the camp."

Gabe slowly lifted his head as he looked at Saint Malo, "I understand. It would be best if we get back on the trail to where we were headed anyway. We thank you for your hospitality," he chuckled, "even though I had to explain a little."

Jean grinned and said, "I am certain it was a lesson well learned. I thank you for not killing them all."

"Well, I hope you folks find the peace and freedom you deserve. You're good people," extolled Gabe. He looked at the crowd that had started away to return to their encampment, then added, "I don't know if our paths will ever cross again, but if they do and we can be of help, we will gladly lend a hand." He shook hands with Jean and turned to gather their gear. Ezra also said his good-byes and joined Gabe in their task. The two friends were silent as they geared up the horses and cleared the camp and Gabe knew there were a lot of conflicting thoughts going through Ezra's mind, but he chose to let his friend work it out by himself. Their friendship could stand a little silence and introspection from time to time and this was one of those times.

23 / Scouts

"These are timpsila cakes. Our men take them on long hunts, and with pemmican, there is little need to cook. They are made with the timpsila root flour and fresh berries and more. You will like them," said Beaver as she lifted the bag to Ezra. The draw string leather pouch was heavy, and Ezra could not keep from having a peek inside. He broke off a piece of one of the cakes, tasted it, smiled broadly, and looked down at Beaver. "That *is* good! Thank you, I will enjoy these!"

She grinned, glanced at Gabe and back at Ezra, "They are for both of you."

Ezra chuckled as he stuffed the pouch in his bedroll, and looking at Gabe said, "Well, maybe I'll let him have one."

"When you return, I will make you more," promised Beaver as she turned away, a coy smile over her shoulder promising nothing but suggesting everything.

Gabe laughed as he looked at his friend, then smacked his hand against his thigh and said, "There it is! Bait's been taken, trap has sprung!"

Ezra scowled, "Well, you have to admit, she's a mighty fine lookin' woman, and she can cook too!"

"Leave it to you to put a priority on the cooking!" answered Gabe as he kicked Ebony into a trot, bringing the lead of the pack horse taut and starting them on the way.

It was late morning when they got their start and by mid-afternoon, they chose to give the horses a breather and fix some coffee to go with the timpsila cakes. They had pointed their horses to the southwest. Big Thunder told them they would come to the Niobrara within a day or two, or they could bear to the west and also reach the same river, just farther upstream. The two men were intent on only one thing, going west. The mountains were west, and they wanted to reach the place where granite peaks touched the blue of the sky.

It was just over a year ago that they left their homes in Philadelphia with high hopes of going to the west and exploring all the unknown territory, especially the mountains known as the Rockies. The year had seemed like a lifetime with all the happenings that started on the Ohio River and the Shawnee and so many different native peoples since that first experience. They had grown and learned, but the greatest lesson was to realize how little they knew and how much they still had to learn. Gabe admitted they had lived more in the past year than any five years before. He chuckled as he looked to his friend, "So tell me you weren't tempted to stay with the Maroons and especially Beaver."

Ezra laughed, "I've told you before, I can resist anything but temptation! And these cakes," holding one up before him, "are mighty tempting!"

"You can always be tempted by anything that pleases your palate, even though yours is not very discerning!" Gabe paused a moment, looking at his friend, "What did you *really* think of the Maroons?"

Ezra breathed deep, reached for the coffee pot to refill his cup, then gazed at his friend as he thought. "When any man is brought face to face with his mortality and he is over-whelmed with feelings of futility, I can understand when he grasps at anything that might give him hope."

Gabe frowned, leaned forward to look more closely at his friend, "You've really been giving this a lot of thought, haven't you?"

"That's right. I couldn't help but look at those people, I mean really look, deep into their hearts and souls. Most of them have never known a day's worth of true freedom, not like you and me, and it has probably seemed like an im-possibility, an elusive dream, if you will. They have banded together, found others of like mind and spirit among the native tribes, and now fled across more country than the average person would dare dream about, and they only want freedom. To be left alone to live their lives as they choose, is that so much to ask?" inquired Ezra.

"No, not at all, and in a small way, we can understand. Af-ter all, isn't that what we're doing, fleeing from Philadelphia and the old man that has put a bounty on our heads? We've been traveling for over a year now and hopefully we've put that behind us, but still it's possible that we could wake up one day staring down the muzzle of a rifle in the hands of a bounty hunter. Most of those among the Maroons are no different. They have bounties on them, according to what their leader, Jean, said before we left. So, yeah, I can sort of understand what they're feeling. Tell me, were you tempted to stay with them? Take yourself a wife like Beaver and build a life with them?"

Ezra looked down at the tufts of grass between his feet, then up at his friend, "No, I don't think so. I did think about it, but that's not what I want right now. We've got the entire western lands of the Spanish Territory to explore and that's too enticing for me to give up."

Gabe smiled, "Glad to hear it! Wouldn't be the same without you!"

They pointed their horses due south, seeking to find easier going closer to the Niobrara River. The land was drier, the only green showing in the run-off ravines that held winter's snow and kept the moisture well into spring. That green was dark with the deep colored juniper contrasting with the lighter greens of buttonbush and other shrubbery. Those ravines stood out like dark jagged scars pointing to the dry flat lands. With travel easier on the flats, enough graze offered with the Buffalo, Indian, and Gramma grasses, they made good time, even though they weren't on any schedule.

As the sun searched for a resting place beyond the rolling hills in the west, the men saw the promised green of the Niobrara and kicked their horses to a trot. Camp for the night was an enticing grassy flat nestled between the gravely sand-bar of the river and the cluster of cottonwood at the bank. Ample dry driftwood had stacked at the bend of the river, probably from the highwaters of spring runoff, and the men soon had the makings of a comfortable camp.

With dusk dropping its curtain, Gabe said, "I'm gonna go hunt for some fresh meat. You can fill up on those cakes, but I need some red meat!"

"You go right ahead. I'll get the coffee goin' and maybe some Johnny cakes, you bring some nice backstrap and we'll have us a feast!" answered Ezra.

Gabe snatched up his bow and quiver, checked the loads in his belt pistol, and started out upstream, hoping to catch a nice tender doe coming down to water. He picked his way through the cottonwoods, alder, chokecherry and more, moving as quiet as a lynx on the hunt. After about two hun-dred yards he came to a likely spot where a couple game trails came from the dry hills to the river. It was a place of easy access, a few willows and other brush for cover, but nothing to keep game from the sandbar and the water.

Gabe picked a scraggly bur oak for cover, nocked an arrow and took a knee to wait. The slight breeze was to his face, moving downstream, and stirring the leaves just enough to cover any slight movement he would make. He waited. With shallow breaths and moving only his eyes, his patience was soon rewarded. Movement showed beyond the willows as a doe stepped out, followed by another, then a button buck, another doe, and a larger buck with antlers just forking and still in the velvet.

Gabe waited, if he took his shot too soon, the others would not get their needed water, but too late and he wouldn't get his fresh meat. The does drank, then the button buck, and finally the big buck. With four noses in the water, the button buck jerked his head up, startling the others, but they did not move. The young buck was looking downstream, past Gabe, having probably heard something from their camp. Maybe Ezra had banged a pan on a rock. The nervous deer turned and started back on the trail. Gabe brought the arrow to full draw and let it fly. The feathered missile found its mark just behind the front leg of the button buck and buried itself up to the fletching in his chest. The buck stumbled, and dropped on his neck, startling the others making them take flight and bound through the brush and trees to disappear in an instant. Gabe watched the downed deer, walked slowly to its side, poked its neck with his toe, and satisfied it was dead, he dropped to one knee to begin dressing it out.

Dusk had yielded its shadowy glow to the beginning of night. The stars were lighting their lanterns and the moon, waning from full, hung its speckled orb just above the tree-tops. Gabe had the carcass over his shoulders, one hand holding a front and a back leg, the other carrying the bow as he moved soundlessly through the shadows. He knew he was nearing their camp by the smell of wood smoke, but he stopped, listening. Voices came from beyond the trees, more than one, unfamiliar and speaking what sounded like Spanish.

Gabe dropped to one knee, slid the deer from his shoulders and nocked an arrow. With his usual stealthy moves, he came nearer the camp, always keeping a tree or brush between him and the clearing. He paused, listening, hearing the talk in Spanish which he understood clearly and didn't like what he was hearing.

"Admit it! You are both escaped slaves!"

"No habla español!" declared Ezra. Though Gabe knew Ezra spoke Spanish, he now knew he was up to something. Ezra was held by two men, with a third holding a pistol on him. Gabe knew it would usually take more than two men to hold Ezra, but with the pistol pointed at him, he was biding his time, probably waiting for Gabe to return.

Gabe scanned the camp, four horses were standing, tethered at the far edge, that meant there was a fourth man, but where? He looked, waited, unmoving. Then a fourth man stepped from the trees, fussing with his britches, apparently having gone to the trees to relieve himself. Gabe looked back at the man with the pistol who stood leaning back against the single ponderosa at the camp's edge. All four men were dressed alike, all dark skinned, black hair, and unmistakably mixed race or Spanish. *These must be some of the Soldado de cuera that were chasing the Maroons!* thought Gabe. He chuckled to himself, seeing each of the men sporting their multi-layered leather cloaks that protected them from the arrows of the natives, but wouldn't hardly slow the penetration of an arrow from his Mongol bow.

The men chattered at one another, all talking at once,

gesticulating violently, but it was obvious they wanted to finish with Ezra. Gabe understood one to say, "All we need are his ears! That will get us the reward from the Capitan!"

"But if he is not a slave?" asked another.

"Who will know? You can't tell from his ears if he is free or slave!"

The pistol holder had leaned back against the tree, pistol at his side, one leg cocked up to put his foot against the trunk. He waved the pistol at Ezra and asked again, "You are a slave, no?" Ezra shook his head, doing his best to look confused and not understanding.

Gabe couldn't wait any longer, he could tell the others were at the point of finishing this game. He slowly stepped from behind the tree, bringing the arrow to full draw, and let it fly. His chosen mark was the man with the pistol and the arrow went as bidden. With a whisper, the shaft drove the arrowhead into the trunk of the ponderosa, less than an inch below the man's crotch.

The soldier's eyes flared, a scream sounded as he stared at the arrow, afraid to move, and his britches darkened with urine as he held his breath. He looked where the fletching of the shaft pointed, and saw Gabe step clear, another arrow nocked and at full draw.

Gabe shouted in Spanish, "Drop it! The next one will be in your throat!" He looked from one man to the other, slowly moving his arrow side to side, covering all four men. Ezra suddenly flexed his arms and brought the two men holding him crashing into one another, their heads cracking together with a dull thud that dropped them both to the ground. The fourth man, who had been seated by the fire, stood and grabbed for his pistol, but the arrow pierced the leather cloak and buried itself to the fletching. The man looked down at the feathers, started to lift his head to see his assailant, but fell forward on his face to lie still. The man with the pistol had dropped it at his feet as Gabe commanded, but he reached for it and brought it up, cocking it as he stood, but was staring at the pistol in the hand of Gabe as he walked toward the startled man. The soldier froze, the pistol pointing at the ground at his feet and loosened his grip to let it fall. The cocked pistol discharged, sending the lead ball into the man's leg and dropping him to the ground.

Ezra looked from one of the men to the other and stepped away from the two at his feet who were now stirring and holding their heads. Ezra bent to retrieve the pistols from their belts before they were fully conscious. He walked to Gabe, looked back at the three men, and said, "What took you so long?"

"I had to dress out my deer. Then I sat down to enjoy the sunset for a while and took my time gettin' back, enjoying the cool of the evening, you know how it is when you're all alone in the woods." He looked at Ezra, grinning, "'sides, there were only four of 'em. Why'd you let 'em get ahold of you like that?"

Ezra chuckled, shaking his head, "Just wanted to see what they were up to."

"And just what is that?"

"They're lookin' for the Maroons," explained Ezra.

24 / Report

"Such as it is, the map's purty close. This river here, it's called the White, goes more to the north about here." The scout, Estavanico, jabbed his finger at the map. "This country 'round here's purty mean, lotsa gullies, steep ravines, thick timber in the canyons. This area," pointing a little to the south, "is table land, and lotsa draws and gullies drop off into a valley, 'bout here. That's where the camp is, wide valley, water, right purty place it is."

Capitan Cerranza examined the map, looked at his scout, "From here?" asking for time and distance to their quarry. Lieutenant de Vaca stood to the side, silently observing and learning. He had proven himself an avid student of all things and now sought to learn from his commander about pursuing your opponent.

The scout looked back at the map, pointed, "This here's flat an' easy goin', but oncet we get chere," pointing to the northern area, "it gets rough. But if we got an early start, we could make it by dark, too late to mount an attack, but we'd be there," explained the scout.

"How many of 'em are left?" asked the Capitan.

"Most of 'em, but while I was watchin' there was a white man had a scuffle with some and one of 'em was kilt. They run off the white man and his colored friend. I'd guess there was thirty colored men, 'nother fifteen Injuns able to fight. But they got 'em some women, colored and Injun. They might fight too."

"Humph, the only thing they're good at is running! It won't be any different than when Malo's father was caught. He was hung and so will the son." The Capitan seemed to forget the man he was talking to was a colored. Because Estavanico had a Portugese name and had served the soldados for so long and so faithfully, he was thought of as one of them. Estavanico was a freed slave though, the son of slaves, and no matter how long he had served the soldados as a scout, the bitter resentment of his time in slavery had never lessened. His owner had been from Portugal and was the town blacksmith, a trade he tried to force on Estavanico, and when his owner took sick, he gave Estavanico his freedom, but his memories were strong and often relived. The scars on his back told of his master's whip and the brands on his chest and shoulders came from the hot iron in the forge at the smithy. Brands that had been inflicted to prove the ownership of the blacksmith.

Estavanico turned away from the Capitan to hide his flaring temper, breathing deeply and letting the anger still.

As he turned back to face the commander, the Capitan asked, "Does the camp have easy access?"

"I was on a point south o' the camp. It looked to me like there was access from either end of the valley, but them other ravines were too steep and timbered." Estavanico was looking down at the map, keeping his eyes from the Capitan. He knew there were other ways out of the valley and thought the Maroons and the others would have an easy escape, but in battle, nothing is certain. He was struggling with his own decisions. Although a reward of one hundred pesos was offered for each Maroon, he was also sorely tempted to join them. When he watched them in their camp, he saw a freedom that he did not have, even though he was freed. The restrictions placed on him by the soldados were almost as constricting as those he knew as a slave. The Maroons, they knew the taste of real freedom and all he had to do was join them. He remembered watching the Indian woman that cooked the meal for the white man and his friend. She was a woman that could make a man happy for a lifetime.

He shook his head and looked at the Capitan, "What'd you say, Capitan? I was looking at the map and remembering the country. What was it?"

"I asked if the other scouting patrols were back yet."

"Uh, I'm not rightly sure, sir. They should be, but I didn't see any of 'em."

"Find out. And if any are back, send them in to me, pronto!" commanded the officer.

Estavanico flipped back the flap of the Capitan's shelter

and almost ran into two of the scout band leaders coming to give their report. Sergeant Valazquez and Corporal Iglesias stepped back and nodded to the scout. He growled at them, "The Capitan is waiting for your report. Where's the other one?"

The Sergeant answered, "He is not back yet," and received a nod from the scout as he turned away to give his report.

Estavanico's camp was in the trees, away from the others but nearest the group of coloreds who also kept to themselves. He rolled out his blankets and readied his gear for an early start, was about to stretch out when he heard a commotion in the camp. He craned around to see through the trees and saw some riders coming into camp. He picked up his rifle and started toward the disturbance but as he neared he saw it was the last of the scout patrols returning. This one led by Corporal Lorenzo Dominquez. Since he was here, he thought he'd see if they had found the camp of the Maroons or any other sign.

It was quickly apparent the ruckus was due to the dead body draped over the last of the horses. The body was one of their own and the men were riled. This was not supposed to happen. They were the greatest horsemen in the world and the most feared soldiers. Their cloaks, chaps and shields were to protect them in battle and here this man hung, an arrow protruding from his back, an arrow that had pierced the multi-layered cloak that was supposed to repel the arrows of these plains Indians. The chatter of the men increased when the body was taken down and lay on its back, showing the arrow had penetrated the cloak and the body before exiting the back. With only the fletching showing at the man's chest, the men were surprised to see any arrow that had that power behind it.

Estavanico looked at Corporal Dominguez, "The Capitan wants to see you now."

The Corporal, eyes wide, shook his head and started for the Capitan's tent. Estavanico followed. When the Corporal scratched at the tent flap, he heard the voice of the Capitan, "Entrar!" He bobbed his head and pulled the flap back to enter, saw the scout following and held the flap for him and both entered together.

"Ahh, Corporal Dominguez, good of you to join us! What is your report?"

"We were attacked by a band of Maroons. We fought bravely, I was wounded," he pointed at his bloody pants leg, "and Private Muñoz was killed. We managed to escape after dark and return."

"How many attacked you?"

"We couldn't count exactly, but I would say at least ten or twelve. There was a white man with them, a man armed with a bow that shot an arrow and killed the Private."

The Capitan scowled, looking from the Corporal to his scout and back. "A white man? With a bow? Are you saying there was a white Indian with the Maroons?"

"Uh, yes sir, that's right sir," replied the Corporal, standing at attention and not looking directly at his commander.

"And how were these Maroons armed?"

"Uh, with rifles and pistols," he pointed again to his wound.

"And they only scored with one shot? That's incredible!"

"Uh, you said yourself they were not good soldiers, sir."

The Capitan shook his head, "Yes, I said that." he turned to look at Estavanico, "Do you believe this report, scout?"

"No sir. There was only one white man and his colored friend that left the village. None of the Maroons followed and none left the camp. I stayed till dark last night, and no one left."

The Corporal's eyes grew wide as he looked at the scout, then to the Capitan, and stuttered, "There musta been others, cuz we were attacked!"

The Capitan stood, clasped his hands behind his back, and walked closer to the Corporal. He stood directly before him, looked straight into the man's eyes and spoke quietly, "I believe there were no Maroons, and you probably attacked the white man and his friend, thinking you would get the bounty of one hundred pesos by claiming the colored man was a Maroon and a runaway slave. But they were too much for you and you had to make up this story to cover your mistake. Isn't that so, Corporal? And before you answer, remember the penalty for lying to your superior officer is forty lashes." The Capitan stepped back, watching the Corporal squirm a little and waited. "Well?"

The Corporal fidgeted, dropped his head and mumbled, "Yes sir. That's what happened." Then he looked up, "I didn't think you'd believe me if I said his arrow went through the cuero!" he grabbed at his leather cloak to pull it away from his chest to emphasize what he meant.

The Capitan's eyes flared, and he turned toward the man, growling, "Are you saying one arrow went all the way through the cloak?"

"Yessir, it did sir!" answered the Corporal, obviously nervous at the Capitan's response.

"I'll have to see this!" he stated as he grabbed his hat and started from the tent, pushing the others aside as he stormed out.

The body of Private Muñoz lay where it fell, the men still standing around and talking, obviously upset at seeing their armor ineffective against the arrow of an enemy. The Capitan dropped to one knee beside the body, looked at the fletching of the arrow, then rolled the man to the side, to see the broken shaft protruding from the back. He felt the leather beside the shaft, dropped the body to its back and examined the leather beside the fletching. He pulled back the cloak, feeling the thickness of the multi-layered leather, and stood, still looking down at the dead man. He shook his head, said nothing, and turned away to go to his tent. He hollered over his shoulder, "Get that man buried!"

The Lieutenant followed the Capitan into the tent and asked, "What now, Capitan?"

"What now? We'll do just as we said since we started this campaign. We move out first thing in the morning. The scout knows where the Maroon camp is, and we will take it as planned! When we're done with those runaways, the trees will be decorated with their bodies and their heads will line the trail, just like they did at Pointe Coupée!"

At the mention of the word, the Lieutenant remembered seeing the gruesome sight along the road at Pointe Coupée, the site of a slave rebellion that resulted in twenty-three slaves hung, then decapitated and their heads used to decorate the roadways as a warning to other slaves. Thirty-one more were flogged and sentenced to hard labor and three white men that were a part of the rebellion were deported and sentenced to six years hard labor in Havana. The Lieutenant shook his head as he left the tent, not wanting to see history repeat itself.

25 / Considerations

"I don't think we shoulda let 'em go!" declared Ezra, watching the three soldados ride into the dark.

"They won't be back," responded Gabe. "They'll be licking their wounds for a while and don't want any more of what we gave 'em."

"That's not what I was thinkin'. They were lookin' for the Maroons and with other scouts out, they might find 'em. After what that corporal said, there's a whole company of 'em and their captain is dead sure he's gonna find 'em, and they ain't that hard to find!"

Gabe leaned back against the log, holding the last of the coffee in the steaming cup before him and looked at his friend, "Look Ezra, they've come all the way from New Orleans without our help, I'm pretty sure they can handle this on their own. 'Sides, what can the two of us do against a whole company of Spaniard Soldados?"

"Since when has bein' outnumbered ever stopped you?"

"Well, you're the one that's always complaining about me gettin' us into trouble!" answered Gabe. He was pushing Ezra for the fun of it. He had already decided to do what they could to at least warn the Maroons, if not help them against the Soldados, but the two friends had a life-long habit of pushing one another into any adventure that arose.

"Alright! So, it's my turn to get us into trouble, so be it!" declared an exasperated Ezra, throwing his hands up and grabbing up his cup of coffee that sat waiting on the fireside rock.

"So, whaddya wanna do? Warn 'em, scout 'em, or fight 'em?" asked Gabe, grinning.

Ezra looked at his friend, saw the laughter in his eyes and picked up a stick to throw at him before he answered, "All of it! Ain't that what we do best?"

They kept to the bottom edge of the bluffs where the rolling hills flattened into the grassy bottomland of the Niobrara Riverbed. Following the downstream flow took them into the morning sun, but the plan was to search for any sign of other scouts from the soldados that might have come closer to the Maroon camp. Knowing the troops were bivouacked somewhere south of the Niobrara and probably closer to the North Platte would necessitate any scouts to cross the Niobrara to locate the encampment of the Maroons. The corporal that led the scout that attacked them the night before had said, upon threat of letting him bleed to death, that there were two other scout patrols and a single scout that were also looking for the encampment.

Ezra had taken the lead and the pair had been on the move for about three hours before he reined up, leaning off the side of his mount and searching the ground. He stepped down and went to one knee, reaching down to examine some tracks in the moist soil. He stood, looking back at Gabe, "These are 'bout three days old, shod, long stride, headin' due north. One horse, could be that of the single scout."

"Sounds right, but if he found something, or even if he didn't, we should find another set where he returned," suggested Gabe. "Don't chu think?"

"Yeah, I reckon. Most seasoned scouts wouldn't follow the same trail back, so, mebbe we'll cross them a little further on," surmised Ezra, swinging back aboard his bay. They had gone less than a hundred yards when Ezra stopped and stepped down again. He looked to the ground, stood and grinned at Gabe, pointing to the tracks, "And here they are! Same horse, last night, going due south. Movin' faster, probably has some news to report."

"Best way to tell that is to back track him. That'll tell us a lot," said Gabe, looking back to the north across the band of bluffs, knowing the flats were beyond before they would reach the rugged hills that cradled the encampment of the Maroons. "Let's give the horses a breather, get some coffee, and then we'll push 'em a little harder back north."

Moving at a canter, a trot, then a walk and back again, they pushed the mounts through much of the afternoon. With a

brief rest, they came to the long line of rimrock that marked
the edge of the flat top overlooking the myriad of timber
lined valleys. They pushed off the edge, following much the
same course that Big Thunder led them on their first visit,
and taking the faint trail to the point above the valley. The
tracks of the scout, if they were the scout's, took them to the
same promontory. The two stepped down and searched the
area, reading the tracks as clear as a painted sign, that told of
the scout's brief stay and watching the camp below.

"'peers to me he was here more'n a day. Wouldn't surprise
me if he was watchin' while we were here," observed Ezra
as he pointed to the edge of the camp where they had spent
the night. "He was here long 'nuff to know a lot about the
camp and the people." Ezra was an educated man and could
fluently speak the King's English,, but he, like most of the
men in the wilderness, found it easy to lapse into the vernac-
ular of the time and country. When the priorities of a man
turn from appearances and manners to survival and living,
the thoughts and tongue of that same man become lazy or at
least lackadaisical.

Gabe pointed to the edge of the promontory where a
stretch of soft soil held tracks and more, "He has a scope.
See there, both his elbows were on the ground while he lay
stretched out on his belly for a spell. He was watchin' 'em
close."

"Reckon so. What now?" asked Ezra. Both men looked
to the west, judging the light left in the day, then with a nod
and a motion, Gabe mounted up to be followed close behind

by Ezra. They pushed off the point and started for the camp, staying in the clear, hands visible, showing no threat. Within moments, a warning came from the trees, "Hold up! Lift your hands high!"

Both men stopped, dropped the reins on the necks of their mounts and lifted their hands. Ezra spoke, "We're here to see Jean, your leader!"

Two men stepped from the trees, both holding rifles trained on the visitors and one man said, "I know you! You're the one fought Parkinson!"

"That's right," answered Gabe. "But we've got news for Jean, urgent news."

"You weren't supposed to come back. A man was killed cuz o' you. We're not supposed to let exiles back into the camp."

Ezra looked hard at the man, "Send your friend there to tell Jean we're here. If he don't want us, we'll leave, but if we do, you might not live another day!"

The man's eyes flared, and he stepped closer, lifting his rifle toward Ezra, "Are you threatenin' me?" he growled.

"Nope, just tellin' you how serious and urgent this message is for Jean."

The man glared at Ezra and back to Gabe, then stepped back and nodded to his partner to go tell Jean. He motioned the men to step down, warning, "I'll kill the first one that tries anything!"

Within moments, Jean, followed by a small group of armed men, came before Gabe and Ezra, scowling, asking,

"Why have you returned? You were told you would no longer be welcome!"

Gabe stepped forward, lifted his head, "Those Soldados you said you fought back in New Orleans? They're about a day's ride from here!" He paused a moment as the news struck the leader like a fist in his gut, then continued, "You had a man up there on that promontory," he pointed behind him, "who has been watching you for the last couple days. He's gone to report to the Capitan of the company of Soldados and I reckon they'll be comin' along pretty soon."

One of the men behind Jean stepped forward and snarled, "Why would you warn us? What do you care what happens to us?"

Gabe recognized the malcontent immediately as the man he fought with, James Parkinson. Gabe shrugged his shoulders, "Seemed like the right thing to do, if you can understand that."

Jean shouldered James aside, "How soon do you think they'll be here?"

"I figger you've got at least a day, not much more," answered Gabe.

"How many are there?"

"The man said there was a company, near as I can tell, about forty men."

"What man?" asked James, stepping forward again. "You were talking with them?" He turned to Jean, "They're in it with them! This is a trap!"

Ezra spoke up, "A scouting party, four men, jumped me when we were camped. They wanted to kill me, cut off my ears, and turn them is as if from a runaway slave and collect the bounty. We fought, killed one, let the others go after we found out what we could."

"They probably told them where our camp was! They need killing!" threatened Parkinson.

Gabe looked at him, "We didn't need to tell them anything, they had a scout watching your camp for the last two days, like we said!" Gabe looked from Parkinson to Jean, "We've done what we set out to do. You've been warned and since we're not welcome, we'll be on our way."

Parkinson jumped toward Gabe, holding a pistol and threatening, "They're goin' to tell the soldados!"

Without an instant's hesitation, Gabe backhanded the man, grabbed his pistol as he fell and tossed it aside. He stepped next to the man, leaned over him slightly and glared at him, "I've had it with you. You threaten me again and you'll be pickin' lead outta your teeth!" He stepped back, looked at Jean and mounted Ebony, reined him around and jerked at the lead line of the packhorse and started back up the draw toward the flat-top. Ezra looked from Jean to the retreating Gabe, swung aboard his bay and with lead rope in hand, followed his friend into the trees.

They stopped when they came to the promontory that overlooked the camp, Gabe looked below, shook his head and reined Ebony around, but was stopped by Ezra. "Are you gonna let that snake win?"

Gabe scowled, "Whaddaya mean?"

"If we leave now with our tails tucked between our legs,

you're letting that scum think he chased you out. That's not like the Gabe I know."

Gabe breathed deeply, looked at his friend, "I know, but if I'da stuck around I probably would have ended up killin' him and I've had enough of that."

"You haven't killed anybody that didn't need it! 'Sides, you and I both know there's gonna be more before we get done with our 'exploring' the wild country. I think it was you that quoted a fella named Burke that said, 'The only thing necessary for the triumph of evil is for good men to do nothing.'"

Gabe glared at his friend, shook his head and grinned. Ezra knew that Edmund Burke was a man often praised by Gabe. He had been a long-time member of British Parliament and an advocate of the American Colonies. His views expressed in his writings had struck a familiar chord with Gabe, who had read everything written by the man, but to be called to account in regard to his basic beliefs, here in the middle of the unsettled wilderness, and by his best friend, gave Gabe pause. "Alright, alright, you can quit'cher preaching!"

Ezra grinned, "That was a purty good sermon, wasn't it?" He chuckled, then asked, "So, what're we gonna do?"

The two stepped down and looked at the valley below. They were on a promontory that sat between two draws that came together in a confluence that formed a wider green valley that held the encampment. The draw to the right, about a hundred fifty feet below them, held a small stream that fed the valley. Beyond it rose a long ridge that formed the east wall of the valley. To their left, a series of timber covered buttes and hills walled in the west edge of the same valley. Beyond the encampment, another valley came from the west to make a dogleg with the larger green bottomed valley and offered a way of escape, similar to the north end of the basin that led away.

"If I was leading the attackers, I'd have some men take that west vale there, while I took this one below us, and we'd attack from both directions at the same time. Maybe even have some on that north fork yonder." He paused, considering, "Now, if I was there," pointing to the east ridge, "I could see both approaches with my scope and know when they were gonna hit, and maybe give some kinda warning. Then I'd move around behind this bunch and come at 'em from the flank, and if I hit 'em just before they hit the camp, it'd confuse 'em enough to give the Maroons advantage." He thought some more, visualizing his plan and looking at the terrain. "And maybe if you were to take a spot there, on that hilltop at the end of the west valley, you could come at that bunch on their flank, just like here."

"And if Jean had his men, split to come head-on at both forces, maybe some from the sides yonder, it'd be a right fine ambush. Yessir," declared Ezra.

26 / Groundworks

The tall trees on the valley floor that lined the creek stretched their shadows up the hillside, chasing the remnants of the day's sun into retreat. Gabe and Ezra made their camp on the west slope overlooking the village of the Maroons. After their strategy session, Ezra had gone into the encampment to talk with Jean Saint Malo while Gabe made camp. Now the two men sat watching the strips of venison broil over the flames, dripping their juices into the coals. It was not their custom to stare into the fire as most lonely men do, preferring to preserve their night vision. This was the eve of what promised to be an extraordinary battle, and no man's tomorrows are guaranteed, even those intent on doing right by their fellow man. Right or wrong, a lead ball or sharp tipped arrow shows no preference nor discrimination.

Gabe picked up his coffee, took a long draught and looked to Ezra, "So, Jean likes our plan, does he?"

"Ummmhummm. Course, he's got a few ideas of his own.

He's gonna send a man up here to join you and one with me. Don't know what good they'll do, but maybe watch our back."

"He tell you what other ideas he has?"

"No, but he grinned a little like he's lookin' forward to it. I think they've been in a scrap or two their own selves," surmised Ezra.

"Prob'ly. Way I understand it, most of those folks have been fightin' all their lives," remarked Gabe.

They soon finished their meal of venison steaks and left-over Johnny cakes, and set about cleaning and readying their weapons. Gabe's dad had always insisted he have a spare rifle and there were two among the packs. Gabe handed one to Ezra and asked, "You want another pistol?"

"Nah, I've got my turnover like yours, and with this spare rifle, and my war club, that's enough to keep me busy. You know me, I like the close in work best."

Gabe chuckled, "Maybe you can keep you helper busy loadin' for you."

"Now there's an idea. Don't know who Jean's gonna send with us, but that'd keep 'em outta trouble, if they know how to load, that is."

Gabe had finished cleaning and loading his Ferguson rifle, leaned it against the log he sat on, and reached for the two French double-barreled saddle pistols and his Bailes turnover double-barreled belt pistol. As both men busied themselves at their task, their pre-occupation allowed a visitor to surprise them until they heard, "Have you had your meal?"

It was Beaver Woman and another woman that stepped into the ring of light, smiling. Ezra was quick to answer, "If you wanna call it that. We had some meat and cornbread and coffee, nothin' like you fix."

Beaver smiled and came closer, "This is Yellow Bird, she is also Lakota, from the Brule. We were sent by JeanSaint-Malo to help you. Whatever you need, we will do." Both women had bedrolls over their shoulders and obviously were prepared to spend the night.

Ezra looked at Beaver Woman and asked, "You wouldn't happen to have some more of those timpsila cakes, would you?"

Beaver smiled and dropped her bedroll, unrolled it a little and brought out a leather pouch, which she handed to Ezra. He grinned widely and said, "Just what I needed, thank you!" He reached into the pouch and brought out a cake and bit into it, smiling and nodding.

"Hey! You're supposed to share those!" declared Gabe stepping closer and reaching for the bag, which Ezra pulled away, shaking his head.

"Humnumm, these are mine!" declared Ezra, holding the bag out of Gabe's reach.

"What kinda friend are you?!" pouted Gabe, scowling and looking away, only to turn suddenly and grab the bag from his friend's hand. He stepped back, grinning and reached into the pouch for a treat of his own. He withdrew a couple, tossed the bag back to Ezra and turned to Beaver, "Thank you, Beaver. These are very good!"

As Gabe walked back into their camp, Beaver and Yellow Bird looked up from their makin's to smile as he came near. Bird asked, "See anything?"

"Yeah, found their camp," he was interrupted as Ezra also stepped near. It was about an hour before first light, Gabe had done his reconnoiter by the light of the low-hanging half-moon and the bright starlight. The beacons of the night still signaled their presence with unwavering clarity in the dark stillness. He had moved silently in the night, returning near their previous promontory and found the camp of the soldados far back and at the edge of the drop-off from the flat top. They had made camp in the edge of the trees and cared little for anything but their own comfort. Several warming fires blazed, men spoke loudly, and no guards had been posted. Whether it was from wilderness stupidity or indifference for the Maroons, it was presumptuous for them to believe they were in no danger or that the Maroons would not know of their presence. The inherent attitude of superiority of those with high breeding such as the Criollos and their consequent disdain for those of lower station had led many rulers into a situation of comeuppance, usually at considerable cost to others.

Gabe crept near, wanting to learn as much about the soldados as possible. The men were turning in for the night, none showing concern for the events of the coming day. He heard bits and pieces of conversations, most bragging about what they planned to do in the coming battle.

"I shall kill cinco!" bragged one man, prompting others to laugh and add their numbers. "Ahh, I shall kill ocho!" countered another. "If you," motioning with a swinging motion of his arm toward the group of four near the fire, "Are going to kill that many, there will be none left for me, so, I will stay here in camp and take a siesta! Don't shoot too loudly to wake me!" chuckled another.

It was obvious to Gabe these men were experienced fighters, for with all the braggadocio they still tended to their weapons and kept them close. He moved away from the bivouacked men and worked nearer the only tent. These were the officers and other leaders, most sitting quietly and staring at the flames. The Capitan spoke to his junior officer, "Lieutenant de Vaca, you and your men should get some sleep, you will be leaving in about two hours," he looked to the sky to guestimate the time until first light. "It will take you about two hours to get in position."

"Si, mon Capitan. We will be ready," replied de Vaca.

"Remember, you are there to prevent their escape! We will attack from the south first and when they flee from us, then, and only then, do you and your men open fire!"

"Si, si. But if you catch them asleep, they will not be able to run!" replied the Lieutenant, shrugging his shoulders and holding his hands palm out below his waist. He was grinning and added, "All we will have to do is bury them."

"We won't bury anybody. We'll leave the cowards for the buzzards and coyotes," spat the captain.

With the angry mood descending on their leader, the

others stood to leave. He paid little attention to them as they turned away to retreat to their blankets. He mumbled, "These wretched cowards have kept me from my woman too long! This miserable country is worse than purgatory!" He poked a stick in the coals to stir up the fire, watched the sparks rise to the darkness and leaned back to stew in his misery alone.

As Gabe related his findings to the women and Ezra, he looked to his friend and asked him and Beaver to take word to Saint Malo about the plan of the soldados. Beaver asked, "Will you be here when we return?"

Gabe looked at Ezra and back to Beaver, "You will not return here. You will go with Ezra to load his weapons for him and Bird will come with me."

The women had prepared some fried patties similar to potato cakes, but they used timpsila and cornmeal with an assortment of fresh-picked berries. They lay the cakes on a plate, hurriedly stacked the rest of the gear and bedrolls under the trees, and each grabbed a couple cakes and started to their chosen place.

Gabe and Bird worked their way through the thick trees to the top of the knoll that overlooked the village and the valley. Gabe went to his chosen point atop an outcropping of moss-covered rock, shielded by a scrub cedar. He slipped the brass telescope from its case and after a quick glance to the east, he stretched out on the cool rock. It was still too dark to use the scope, but his eyes were well adjusted to the dim light and he searched for movement. Even in the darkness, the movement of a company of soldiers would be easily spotted, but there was none.

The eastern sky was just beginning to show color, a muted gold that faded into the indigo of the night sky, as Gabe searched the valleys and flat tops for the soldados. He had guessed the route the band led by de Vaca would take to make his way to the north end of the canyon, and although the route would be mostly behind the hillocks on the west, there would be stretches of the trail where they could be seen from his high-up promontory. Finally, movement caught his attention, just as the first hint of light showed in the east, it was enough to make silhouettes of the smaller band. Gabe squinted to see better, but they were hard to make out. He tried his scope and saw nothing. But he was certain these were the advance group making their way to the north end of the valley.

He turned back to look toward the camp, no fires showed, no movement near the trees. He searched the sloping butte that led to the point above the junction of the two smaller draws and saw movement. The early morning light bent over the edge of hills and lay across the flat, showing the rest of the company on the move. Gabe turned to immediately signal Ezra and the camp below. He used the wide end of his scope to reflect the rising sun and send the signal to Ezra, then below to the camp.

With the light beginning to break across the land, Gabe lifted his telescope for a better look. He had fashioned a hood of leather that overhung the end of the scope to prevent the same reflection he used for a signal to inadvertently warn the soldados. The company was moving off the slope, taking a trail through the trees as Gabe used a break in the cover to count their number. As they moved, he also noticed the absence of their leader, Capitan de Cerranza. He guesstimated about twenty to twenty-five fighting men plus a couple non-coms that led. Then he turned his scope back up the trail to the flat, saw movement at the familiar promontory, and focused in on the small group. There were the Capitan he saw the night before and two others, one probably a non-com and the other a private or orderly. The captain had taken a seat on the big rock and also had a telescope that he brought out and looked to the valley below, searching the encampment of the Maroons.

Gabe saw what he needed and slipped back behind the tree. Returning his scope to the case, he handed it off to Yellow Bird, "Take care of that, it's important to me!" The case had a long cord and she hung it over her neck and one shoulder, letting it hang at her side. Gabe had also given her a powder horn and possibles bag with patches and balls so she could reload the pistols if necessary. She had the turn-over pistol behind her belt, while Gabe had both saddle pistols behind his. He was fairly weighted down with the two pistols, a tomahawk, two knives,

a quiver of arrows and his bow, and the ever-present Ferguson rifle. He started through the trees, working his way to his chosen shooting positions, followed closely by Yellow Bird.

27 / Ambuscade

The two narrow draws, only one carrying a small live stream, came together at the point below the promontory. The single and narrow valley with the stream meandering lazily through the flat bottom served as a funnel with the trees coming down the hillsides and forcing any travelers, man or beast, to come close together before the valley opened into the flat that held the encampment of the Maroons. The soldados had made their way off the mesa by following the well-used trail to the bottom and now rode in a column of twos through the funnel toward the encampment. It was here that Gabe had chosen his firing positions, but he would not make himself known until after they had passed.

As they moved from the narrows, the soldados drew four abreast, then six, then eight. This was the formation they had used many times before. With their bull-hide shields on their left arms, the long lance in their right, two pistols holstered on their saddles and a smooth-bore rifle in a scabbard under their leg, the men were ready for battle. The horses, experienced in battle and feeling the excitement of their riders pranced nervously, high stepping and chomping at their bits, seeming to march in cadence, pushing their way through the tall grasses and low shrubbery.

Sergeant Velazquez was alone several paces in front of the three ranks of soldados. He held an unsheathed sword at his shoulder as he watched the camp for signs of life. Nothing moved, no fires were smoking, nothing stirred. The quiet of the camp was broken only by the muted thunder of hooves. The sergeant, lifted his sword high, twisted around in his saddle to see the ranks behind him, and shouted, "Listo!," paused only a second, "Cargar!"

The men dug the shank of the dull spurs into the ribs of their horses and the entire company seemed to leap together as the horses dug their rear hooves deep and lunged forward lifting their front hooves off the ground. The men leaned low on the necks of their mounts and the thunder, no longer muted, shook the valley bottom as twenty-four horses dropped their combined weights upon the ground and charged into the camp. The men screamed their war cries as they lowered their lances, searching for a target trying to escape the many lodges. Guided by leg pressure, the horses ran through the tipis and earth lodges, men driving the lance points into the buffalo hide tipis, others rearing up their horses to paw at the earthen lodge doorways. The only target they found was the inanimate objects of tools for living. Within moments, a confused professional soldiers were milling about, asking each other questions, searching for someone, anyone, to quell their blood thirst.

The Soldados congregated in the central compound when a sudden barrage of rifle fire came from the trees, billowing smoke that obscured the sight of the forest and sending lead messengers of death to deliver their sentence. Several men fell from their horses, as their leather armor was punctured and blossomed red. Others whirled around, spurring their horses and jerking at the reins to flee, but a second barrage sounded and more fell from their saddles. One man's foot was caught in the tapaderos and his spooked horse jumped and ran, head between his knees, kicking at the clouds and bucking as he arched his back at the sky. The soldados were expecting their quarry to be armed like the natives with nothing more than bows and arrows, believing their leather armor would protect them, but the multi-layered leather cloaks did little to slow the lead bullets and the sudden blows to their bodies shocked them. They felt their vulnerability at the same instant they recognized the day of their death.

When Lieutenant de Vaca heard the screams and shouts of the attack, he readied his men. They were lined out in two ranks of five, he sat his horse at the lead, sword resting on his shoulder, as he leaned toward the camp, waiting anxiously for any sign that would give him the excuse to charge. He had no intention of missing out on the battle, as he waited for someone to try to flee the encampment. Once he heard gunfire, he gave the order to his men, "Sigueme!" and led the charge into the camp. He leaned forward as he spurred his big black gelding, and the horse responded with a lunge that almost unseated his rider. With his mane flying, his tail high, the battle loving horse charged ahead, but the lieutenant was surprised to see several of his fellow soldados already dead and others fleeing, mounts wandering aimlessly. He saw no dead natives or negroes. He looked around for any Maroons, but seeing none, he started to order the men to charge into the middle of the village but was met with a fusillade of rifle fire. He felt the sudden blow to his chest, looked down to see blood blossoming across the leather cloak, then lifted his eyes to see where the attackers were, but another bullet took him in the throat, making him drop his sabre and fall to the ground, dead before he tasted the dust.

Ezra lowered his rifle, quickly reloading, but watching the action in the camp below him. He had scored two hits, one after the other, on the leader of the second wave. As he watched, the soldados following the downed man, moved about aimlessly, and Ezra noticed a handful of those near the rear were coloreds that had lowered their lances and were doing nothing to aid the rest of the soldados in the attack. As he watched, the coloreds drew together and turned their mounts away, trotting toward the trees. Ezra marked the place they entered the woods in his mind, then looked back at the encampment. No one moved. When the first attackers had turned to flee, they had been met with another barrage of gunfire, but he could not see where they were. With his rifle ready, he motioned with his head to Beaver for her to follow, and they slowly moved to the edge of the trees. He looked again at the camp, and started forward, but remembering those he saw leaving, Ezra thought maybe he should follow and see where they went.

Once the three ranks of men had passed his position, Gabe moved closer to the valley floor, awaiting their return. His plan was to cut off any retreat and he readied himself. Moments later he heard the first volley of rifle fire and he lifted his Ferguson to his shoulder, earing back the hammer. He heard the screams of war cries as they turned to shouts of fear and anguish as the wounded cried for mercy and aid. Then the thunder of hooves told of the retreat and the men coming his way. The first man that appeared was the same man that led them into the fight. Sergeant Valazquez was lying low on the neck of his horse, both hands empty, apparently having lost both his lance and his shield. His wide eyes showed white as Gabe brought the front blade of his sight to bear, but his figure was obscured as the Ferguson bucked and spat lead and smoke. Gabe instantly dropped the rifle from his shoulder, spinning the trigger guard to open the breech. He dropped a ball in the breech, poured in the powder and spun the trigger guard to close it and cut the proper amount of powder. Once the breech was closed, he filled the pan with powder, slapped the frizzen down and lifted the rifle for another shot. It was less than ten seconds since his first shot, and he followed it with another death dealing missile of lead that unseated the second rider. A pistol barked from the brush at the side and another soldado slumped but didn't fall. Gabe knew that was

Yellow Bird exacting her own vengeance.

He quickly pulled the pistols from his belt, lifted one and fired, cocked the second hammer and fired again. He lifted the second pistol, fired twice, and dropped below the smoke to see the results of his shots. Five men lay grotesquely twisted in the grass and brush, and no others came at them. The horses had trotted away, reins dragging, and would be caught later. He motioned to Yellow Bird to join him and started reloading his pistols. When she came near, she dropped to one knee and reloaded the turnover pistol. Gabe looked at her and said, "You check those men, but be careful, they might not all be dead. You do what you think is right, but I'm going up there," he pointed to the promontory at the point of the mesa, "cuz that Capitan is up there and he's the one that started all this."

Bird nodded, and stood to offer the pistol to Gabe, "No, you hold on to that for now. You might need it. I'll get it from you later." She nodded again and started toward the casualties in the grass. When she turned to look back at Gabe, he was gone.

The thunder and rattle of rifle fire echoed across the valley and a low cloud of powder smoke hung lazily as if snagged on the pole tips of the tipis. The sporadic shots lessened and only the whinny of wounded horses and the cries of wounded men was heard. Slowly, shadowy figures came from the trees, rifles held at their shoulders with muzzles down. Both the men and women of the Maroons picked their way through the encampment, checking on each of the downed soldados. Whenever a wounded one showed life, he was either dispatched or brought by force to the central compound with others. When the people gathered, there were six wounded men seated together on the ground, backs to one another, and in the middle of the compound under the guard of several rifle-toting men. The Maroons had caught the horses of the men and now led them into camp, weapons already stripped from the saddles and carried by those that led the horses.

As Gabe came to the top of the mesa that held the overlooking promontory, he paused, staying behind cover of a small juniper. There at the point, seated on the large boulder Gabe had himself used as a lookout point, was Capitan Andrés de Cerranza, mumbling his frustration because the powder smoke from the rifle fire masked his view of the battle. While behind him, Gabe saw three horsemen come from the trees, heading for the previous night's campsite, but their horses were winded and moved at a walk. None of the men looked anywhere but the hoped-for safety of their camp. Beside the captain were two men, one showing chevrons on his left sleeve, the other none. These two men were lackeys, stationed with the captain to tend to his needs as he watched the battle from safety.

Gabe stood, rifle in hand and held across his chest, and slowly walked up behind the trio. While they focused on the scene below, Gabe spoke calmly and in Spanish, "Stand easy!

Drop your weapons!" he ordered.

At his word, all three spun around, the captain staying atop the rock, but the other two quickly raising their hands. If they had any weapons near, he couldn't see them. "Where's your weapons?" he asked.

"No, ninguna. We have no weapons, they are in camp, señor," said the corporal, looking from the private to the Capitan.

The Capitan slipped from the boulder and stood before Gabe, demanding, "Who are you and how dare you to hold a rifle on me! I am Capitan Andrés de Cerranza of the Presidio at Santa Fe. I am on official business and you are interfering! Put that rifle down, now!"

Gabe grinned, chuckled a little, then waved the muzzle of the Ferguson at the Capitan and said, "You are not on any official business anymore. You are my captive!"

"Captive?! I am no one's captive! I order you in the name of the government of Spain and of Spanish Louisiana, put your weapon down! Now!"

Gabe grinned again, noting the sweat showing on the Capitan's forehead. His nostrils were flaring, and the corner of his lip lifted as he snarled. This man was angry and that made Gabe chuckle. "Alright, Capitan. I will put down my rifle," started Gabe, leaning forward to set the Ferguson on its butt plate to lean it against the boulder. He took his eyes away from the three for just an instant, more of an invitation than carelessness, and with his body slightly turned from them, he made his rifle stable with his left hand, but drew a pistol with his right, cocking it as he brought it out but masking the sound with a cough.

As he expected, the corporal lunged for him, but Gabe turned to meet his charge, bringing the barrel of the pistol up under the man's chin and stopping his charge. The man stumbled, waving his arms to keep his balance, hoping Gabe would not pull the trigger and Gabe said, "No, no, no! That's not what I told you to do!"

The Capitan seeing what he thought was an advantage, snarled, "Shoot him! Then you won't have another shot and we," motioning to the private and himself, "will take you and kill you! Now, as I said before, drop your weapon!"

Gabe grinned again, looking at the Capitan. "Oh, but Capitan. You are so mistaken! Didn't you notice? I have another pistol in my belt. Now, you do like I tell you and you might live a little longer."

The Capitan's face dropped, his anger still showing, but his frustration adding to his confusion and he chose to do what he swore he never would and gave himself up to his captor. Gabe looked to the Corporal and private, "You two, there's three or four of your men back at your camp," and was interrupted by the Capitan. "There's no one at the camp! They all went to the battle!"

"No, Capitan, they all ran, at least those few that were still alive, and there's some back at your camp. They are probably getting some supplies to high-tail it outta here." He looked to the two men again, "If you two want to join them, and give your word you won't come back, you can go!"

Both men stammered, looked to the camp in the distant trees and saw horses moving, and the corporal spoke quickly, "We give you our word. We will not return!" Gabe waved with his pistol and the two men started running to the camp without a look back to their Capitan. Gabe grabbed up his Ferguson rifle and motioned the captain before him and they started back to the Maroon encampment.

28 / Trial

Ezra walked behind four men, each leading his horse and walking one behind another, occasionally looking over their shoulder at Ezra, with random glances toward Beaver who also carried a rifle, muzzle toward them as she walked alongside. They walked toward the gathering at the central compound and the Maroons stepped aside as they approached. These men were all colored but wore the uniform of the soldados. They stopped as they came near the leaders who were assembled before the prisoners. Jean looked to Ezra as he came to the front. Ezra nodded, "These four rode into the trees when the battle started. I didn't see them charge or strike anyone. I'm thinkin' they're wantin' to join up with you, but we haven't had time for a heart to heart talk."

Jean looked at the four men, walked from one to the other, then stood back, "Explain yourselves."

The men looked to one another, then one stepped forward, "I am Daniel Wheeler. We," nodding toward the others, "have talked long about this and we would like to join you."

"Why? You don't even know us or what we are doing?" asked Saint Malo.

"We know you are free, and we are not," answered Wheeler. He looked to his friends who nodded in agreement, fidgeting under the stares of the other Maroons.

"You have fought against us, perhaps killed some of our own, and now you think we should take you in, why?"

"We have not fought against you. Our company was in Santa Fe and only fights we have been in were against renegade Apache. We had agreed we would not fight against you or any others of our kind."

A commotion came from the edge of the group as they parted to show another man coming toward them. This man was dressed differently, more like a native, probably an Apache, but he was a colored man. Estavanico carried a rifle loosely cradled in his hand at his side and he spoke confidently, "He speaks the truth. These men have been talking of this since the first day we learned of our assignment. None of us chose this detail. I have fought against the Maroons in the swamps near New Orleans where you come from, but when I learned more about them, I did not fight them. I am a scout and did only as I was ordered. I too, want to join you."

Suddenly a shout came from their perimeter, "Cowards! Traitors! Turncoats! You swore an oath!" The Capitan staggered when Gabe pushed him forward, then he snarled at the people, "Get out of my way you stinking animals!" Several stepped aside to let him through, as others crowded closer to see who was shouting the insults.

Jean and the other leaders turned to face this new interruption and he saw Gabe pushing the uniformed man forward. When they stepped into the fore Gabe said, "Jean, let me introduce you to the leader of this rabble, Capitan Andrés de Cerranza. Capitan, meet Jean Saint Malo, the leader of this band of Maroons." He stepped back, turning the Capitan over to the Maroons.

The captain stood before Jean and the other leaders, moving only his eyes to squint at each one, then with one eyebrow raised, he snarled, "Yes, I am the leader," and lifted his head proudly to look down on those around him. He flared one nostril as he curled his lip in disgust.

"So, you came all the way from Santa Fe just to stand trial before our tribunal?" asked Jean.

The Capitan turned his head slightly to look around, raised an eyebrow and glared at Jean, "You are mistaken. I came to put you on trial and carry out your sentence of death!" he spat the words as he spoke. Contempt was written across his face but there was no fear.

Jean looked directly at the presumptuous potentate before him, "You pompous fool! You thought you were coming against a bunch of rag-tag helpless runaways and your prejudice and arrogance has brought you to this. We counted twenty-three dead, six more here awaiting their trial and you still think you are in command. We are not on trial, you are!" He turned to his circle of leaders, four men, two with salt and pepper hair and ample wrinkles but with life in their eyes, and one woman, matronly, full bosomed and grey haired, whose eyes threw daggers. "How say you?"

Each member of the leadership looked at the Capitan and slowly, one by one, they held out their closed hand, then gave a thumbs down sign. Vote was unanimous and Jean turned back to the Capitan, "Guilty," he glared at the man and continued, "Now, what shall be your sentence?"

A voice came from the group of soldados waiting with Ezra, "He swore he would hang any Maroon that survived the attack. He was ordered to kill or capture each of you. Those that lived were to be taken back and surrendered as runaways, but he swore he would hang any survivors." It was Jedidiah Green, the eldest of the colored soldados that sought to join the Maroons. Every face turned from Jedidiah back to Jean as he stood before the Capitan. Jean looked to Gabe, then to Ezra, and received no response from either man. He looked at the captain who had suddenly lost his bravado as he realized what he was facing. With eyes wide, he breathed deeply, fear painting his face as he heard Jean say, "Out of his own mouth." The Capitan glared at Jean, "You have no authority!"

"These are my authority," said Jean, arms extended as he turned to face his people.

Gabe turned away and walked toward his camp. His rifle cradled in his hand, he stepped into the trees and followed a dim game trail higher to the shoulder where they had camped. He sat down, stirred the coals with a stick and dropped the stick and several others on the beginnings of flame. He pushed the coffee pot closer and rested his elbows on his knees as he stared at the small flames licking at the fresh wood. His mind was empty, and he relished the quiet. He didn't want to think or feel. He was tired, tired of fighting, tired of trouble, tired of conflict. He slowly shook his head and held it in his hands, eyes closed, sitting quiet.

His reverie was stirred when he heard the rattle of the coffee pot, the brew bubbling and making the pot dance on the stone. He lifted his head and started to reach for the pot when he saw Ezra across the fire, sitting against a boulder, looking at him. He reached for a cup, poured it full, offered it to Ezra who gladly accepted it, and poured another for himself. The friends sat in silence, until a meadowlark let loose with his trilling call and both men looked up to see the brilliant yellow and brown bird sitting on a branch high above their heads. He was sounding his call for his mate, who landed nearby and cocked her head to listen to another call.

Both men chuckled, but a voice from behind Gabe said, "That is why they call me Yellow Bird." She had made the second and perfect imitation call. Both birds looked toward the three at the fire and flew off after one another.

"Would you like me to cook you a meal?" asked Bird.

Ezra looked to Gabe and both men grinned as Ezra answered, "I never turn down a good meal!"

They were joined by Beaver who brought a large pouch of timpsila and pitched in to help Yellow Bird prepare the meal. As the women worked, Gabe and Ezra cleaned their weapons, each keeping to his own thoughts until Gabe said, "I let six of 'em go."

Ezra looked up, "You what?"

"I let six of 'em go. Four of 'em had run from the fight and were heading outta the country, but stopped at their camp, probably for supplies, and two were with the Capitan. I told 'em to skedaddle and never come back, so they did."

Ezra looked at him, then back to his rifle laying on his lap, then said, "The five I brought in all wanted to join up, so they were accepted on a trial basis, kind of a probation."

"You think they'll prove out?"

"Probably. They don't have much other choice. If they were to go back, they might be treated as deserters if the word got out about they're not fightin', but I think they'll be alright. They have as much to lose as the rest of 'em." They were interrupted by a call from Beaver that the meal was ready, and they eagerly turned their attention to something more rewarding.

29 / Departure

"I know you think my time in University was fruitless, but I did a lot of study of those that ventured into the western wilderness before us," said Gabe, looking at Ezra. The men were riding west southwest along the same route they started on before their encounter with the scouts from the soldados. It was a beautiful day, not a cloud in the sky and the arching blue canopy so brilliant it almost hurt the eyes. A red-tailed hawk circled overhead sounding its screeching warning to the intruders to his hunting territory. A fox stopped his digging for field mice to look over his shoulder at the passersby and cicadas rattled in the sparse grass.

"There have been many expeditions into this country, going back more'n two hundred years. Hernando De Soto covered the southeast, never coming this far north, but Coronado came from the southwest and explored much of that area. Now, Pedro de Villasur, he did come up this way, but he came from the Santa Fe area and was after French trappers and that was only seventy-five years ago and he and most of his men were killed in the doing of it. The far north has been covered by the trappers from the Hudson's Bay company and the Northwest Company. Then there's those we ran into with the Missouri Company that were headin' up the Missouri, but we don't want to go where the others have been," he paused, and Ezra asked, "We don't?"

"No, of course not. We want to explore where others haven't, isn't that what we always talked about?"

"Yeah, I reckon, but after all you said, is there such a place?" asked Ezra.

"That's where we're headin'. We'll be north of where all those Spanish explorers were, and south of where the Northwest and Hudson's Bay companies have been. We might run into some independent trappers or such, and of course there'll be plenty of natives, but its country we need to explore. Don't you think?" asked Gabe.

"Well, like you said, it's what we've talked about since we was youngin's. So, here's to our dreams!" He lifted his water jug to the air as if making a toast in the finest of restaurants, prompting Gabe to match his action and the two grinning friends toasted their future together.

They crossed the Niobrara, such as it was, now more of a creek than a river, shallow water maybe fifteen feet across. The brilliant colors of the setting sun sent lances of gold and orange across the western sky as the tall prairie grasses waved their goodbyes to another pleasant day on the prairie. The meandering stream offered a wide bed of tall grass bordered by the cottonwood and alder of the stream for a campsite for the two men. The travelers had grown tired after the long day and were anxious for a bit of rest.

As Ebony lifted his head to climb the low bank, he was startled by two young bucks scampering from the willows. Gabe instantly brought his rifle from the scabbard, took aim and fired, dropping the larger of the pair and watched the other buck bound away into the wide stretch of tall grass.

"Good shootin'!" declared Ezra as he pushed his mount from the water. He stepped down beside Gabe, took the reins of Ebony, "I'll tend to the horses, you drag that fresh meat back and we'll enjoy some juicy steaks for supper!"

They hung the carcass from a big limb on the cottonwood and Gabe skinned it out as Ezra, having already stripped the backstrap, hung slices of the choice cut from willow withes dangling over the flames. He had whipped up a batch of cornmeal for Johnny Cakes and had some timpsila baking in the coals. Gabe spoke as he worked, "I figger we can head more west from here. According to what Estavanico said, we should follow the North Platte through Cheyenne and Arapaho country."

"Either of them friendly?" asked Ezra as he checked the broiling steaks.

"Beaver Woman said both are moody. Dependin' on what kinda year they're havin' will tell if they're friendly or not. She said a good huntin' year makes 'em willing to talk and trade."

"I'd just as soon pass 'em on by. We've had more'n our

share of gettin' acquainted with new natives, and ain't all of it been good!"

"I'd hafta agree with you on that. Even the Maroons were less than friendly," observed Gabe. He had stripped the hide down and it lay at his feet. He was cutting the meat from the bone and making a stack on the hide. "After we rest up a mite, maybe we should get back to travelin' at night, least till we get outta Indian country."

Ezra chuckled, "I'm all for moonlight travelin', but what makes you think we'll ever be out of Indian country?"

"Well, I like to at least get where there ain't so many of 'em, or where they're friendly. I reckon all this country has some breed of natives."

"You 'bout done with that meat? Supper's ready!"

Gabe dozed off and on but never dropped into a deep sleep. He stared at the stars, contemplating their future and what they hoped to find. It had never been about finding a fortune or changing the course of their lives, but about seeing new country, experiencing life unlike most of those that spent their time pursuing what some were already calling the American Dream or success in the eyes of their contemporaries. Gabe and Ezra had never been concerned with the approval or acceptance of those around them. They had always focused on doing what they enjoyed and pursuing their own unique dreams of exploring and experiencing more than their friends and family thought possible.

Since Gabe had trusted Christ as his Savior as Ezra had

taught him, his thoughts had been quite different. He had become more concerned about others, not so much what they thought of him, but the needs and welfare of others, more than himself. Since they left Philadelphia, there had been so many occasions where they were put in predicaments that enabled them to do just that, help others. It didn't matter if they were transplants from France like those on the river, or farmers en route to New Orleans on a trading journey, or any of the many tribes of natives, they had been a help to the Osage, the Otoe, the Omaha, and the Maroons. It had never been one-sided, they always learned and benefitted from the friendships, and Gabe considered those friendships a reward of incalculable worth.

He looked at the moon, guessed it to be about midnight, and rolled out of his blankets. He stirred the coals, added a couple sticks, and pushed the coffee pot nearer the small flames. He went to the horses and started saddling Ebony and the big black bent his neck around to get a good look at his friend, but he was as anxious as Gabe to be on the trail. He was a traveling horse and loved being on the move.

Ezra stirred, sat up and stretched, looked at the moon and then at Gabe, "That was a short night!" He crawled from his blankets and joined Gabe by the horses, and geared up his bay, then started loading the pack horses. They took a few minutes to down their coffee, threw the dregs aside and packed the pot. Gabe swung aboard and Ezra quickly followed. Gabe spoke over his shoulder, "With that full moon, we ain't missin' nothin'."

"Ceptin' sleep," grumbled Ezra, slouching in his saddle and letting the rolling gait of the bay give him comfort.

In the east, the low rolling hills were silhouetted against the pale gold of early morning. It was the end of their second night traveling and they came to the bank of a small stream that chuckled its way south. "I think we'll follow this to the North Platte, it shouldn't be too far," declared Gabe, turning the big black to side the creek. He was right. The sun was just bending its bars of gold across the rolling hills when the creek took a dog leg bend and emptied into the much larger North Platte River.

Beyond the tree line, the big river bent around a wide sandbar that harbored a small pool on the upside of the current. The water in the North Platte was not real clear, but the silt had settled in the pool and the clear water was inviting. Gabe looked to Ezra, "I'm thinkin' its time we had us a bath. I'm gettin' to where I can't hardly stand myself, and it's been a long time since I was able to stand downwind of you!"

Ezra feigned shock, lifted his arm as if to sniff his armpit, made a face and said, "Race ya!"

Gabe jumped to the ground, undoing the ties on his britches and reaching for the drawstrings on his tunic. He pushed his moccasins off as he fumbled with the ties and hopped on one foot toward the water. The horses, used to being ground tied watched the unusual antics of their riders with interest, but stayed where they were, each one dropping its head for a mouthful of green grass. The water splashed as

Gabe barely beat Ezra to the pool, but Ezra had dug in the packs for some lye soap and quickly followed his friend into the cool water. They were laughing, splashing, sudsing and scrubbing a few clothes, those that weren't made of buckskin, and enjoying themselves. Then Gabe looked around, looked at Ezra, "Did you hear that?"

"Hear what?"

"Sounded like a rifle shot. Over thataway," nodding his head to the other bank of the river.

Both men listened, and slowly climbed from the pool. They had made an unusual mistake. Their weapons, except for the turnover pistols and hawks they carried in their belts, were on their saddles. They hopped barefooted closer to the ground tied horses, dug the dry set of buckskins from their bedrolls and hurriedly dressed, always watching the far side of the river, expecting a war party of natives to come storming across. All was still though, and the frogs at river's edge croaked while a squirrel scolded them from the cottonwoods. Both men relaxed as they stripped the gear from their horses and began readying their camp. With the sound of rifle fire so close, it didn't promise to be a time of rest and quiet.

30 / Schooling

"Haloo the camp!" came a call that surprised both Gabe and Ezra. They had heard nothing and were busy building drying racks to smoke the rest of the meat from the deer taken by Gabe, and to hear someone call in English was an even greater surprise. Gabe stood and looked across the river to see a man sitting horseback and looking at their camp.

"Come on in if you're friendly!" declared Gabe, and spoke softly to Ezra, "I don't think he saw you, so move back into the trees until we're certain sure about him. Looks to be a trapper." Ezra grabbed up his rifle and in a crouch moved to hide behind some chokecherry bushes, and went to the trees.

The man pushed his mount into the river at the edge of a riffle that marked the gravel bottom. The horse had little difficulty with the water that came just above his knees and he stopped mid-stream to take a long drink. His rider goaded him onward and they rose up on the sandbar and came into the grassy clearing. He looked to Gabe, "Bonjour! I am

Francois LaRamee. I am pleased to see a friendly face. May I get down?"

Gabe motioned him down and said, "I am Gabe Stone. It's a surprise to see you here in the middle of nowhere. Sit, we've got coffee if you'd like."

"Oui, oui. It has been a long time since I had any coffee," he spoke with a strong French accent but was easily understood. "You can tell your friend I am harmless, and he can come out now," grinned the man. He had a full face of whiskers and long hair that hung over his collar, but bright eyes shown from under thick eyebrows and a smile showed even through the mass of mis-directed whiskers. He was of slender build, draped in well used buckskins that showed many swipes of greasy hands on the legs and front. The fringed leggings hung over his beaded moccasins and his red belt held both a hawk and knife in a beaded scabbard. His possibles bag was also decorated with beads and quills, and the powder horn showed intricate carving. LaRamee's fur cap was cocked jauntily to the side and a broken feather stood above the fold. He had laid his flintlock rifle beside him, butt to the ground as he reached for the coffee pot. He had his own enameled cup and poured it full, then brought the aromatic treat to his nose to savor.

He smiled at Gabe and saw Ezra come from the trees, "And what is it that brings you young men into the uncharted wilderness? I don't see any traps so you are not after the beaver, so . . . ?" he let the question hang unanswered as he sipped the coffee. He looked at the two men, smiled and said, "Merci! This is quite an unexpected treat. Merci."

Gabe relaxed a little, sat on the log opposite the coals of the fire and spoke, "You asked what brought us here? As you said, it is uncharted wilderness, and we wanted to see it before everyone came out and tried to civilize it! What about you? Been here long?"

"Oui, this," motioning with his free arm in a wide sweep, "is my home. I have been in one wilderness or another most of my life. I am *a coureur des bois,* I have come from the headwaters of the Missouri River and down the Rocky Mountains. I am on my way back to my home in Canada. I am *Metis.*"

"You're a little far south for a *Metis,* aren't you?" asked Ezra.

"Peut-être, but I was scouting new territory. The Hudson's Bay and North West Companies are crowding out the independent trapper. I was approached by Simon McTavish of the North West Company to scout new territories. I told him I would think about it but decided to make the trip for my own purposes. It is a marvelous country, this land." He took another sip of the coffee, obviously enjoying it greatly.

"But, you apparently haven't been doing any trapping, I don't see any furs," suggested Gabe.

Francois chuckled, looked in his coffee cup and lifted his eyes to the men he considered greenhorns, "But I did have! I had three pack horses, full loaded, until this morning!" He pounded his fist against his leg, scowling. "Them blasted Arapaho! I've been through the land of the Blackfeet, Gros Ventre, Shoshone, Crow and more! Always managed to get through, but these Arapaho!" He spat the expression, shaking his head, "Bunch of young bucks out to prove themselves. Hit me 'fore sunup and came on like a herd o' stampeding buffalo! Worse! They was screamin' and shootin' into ever'thing! I caught one in my leg," he pointed to a dark spot the size of his hand that surrounded a cut in his britches, "There was more'n a dozen of 'em, but I got one, mebbe another'n, 'fore they run off my packhorses. Didn't kill 'em, just drew blood. I had just loaded them pelts on 'em and away they went! They took my ridin' horse too, but the only reason I got him's cuz he's a knob-kneed, long-legged, hammer head and he bites anything or anyone that comes near. He's uglier and meaner than your worst nightmare mother-in-law, and can't nobody stand him but me, and we're best o' friends. He's a mountain-bred mustang and you won't find a better horse than him. He came trottin' back into camp, blood around his mouth, so I know he let one of 'em know what he was thinkin' 'bout them takin' my pelts."

Gabe glanced over at the horse that stood ground tied just beyond the log where his owner sat, and he was almost certain the animal was smiling at his friend. He bobbed his head as if he agreed and let out a little whinny of appreciation or boredom, something to let everyone know he was there.

"See there! He knows I'm talkin' about him," declared Francois, nodding and grinning at his long-time companion.

"We heard a shot early this morning, was that you?" asked Ezra.

"Probably. Them young bucks didn't have no guns of any kind, but they didn't need 'em. They was shootin' arrows so fast I thought it was raining!"

"So, how'd you get away?" asked Gabe, leaning forward in his interest in the man's story.

"Ah, they wasn't interested in scalps, they wanted the pelts and horses. Couple of 'em counted coup on me, but I didn't wanna kill 'em. Once you do that, you've made an enemy! Them boys'll have a lot to brag about and their people will make out they done somethin' special. Those that were shot will tell stories that will grow with every tellin'." He grinned as he thought about it. He had been in many villages and lived among different tribes, but young warriors were all the same, no matter the people.

"Think they've gone very far?" asked Gabe, glancing at Ezra. His friend knew exactly what he was thinking and hung his head, shaking it slowly side to side, knowing Gabe was about to get them into trouble again.

"Non. They'll go a little way, stop and go through the packs to divvy things up. When they see the trade goods, they'll argue and fight about them a while to decide who gets what. It'll take 'em a while." He frowned, looked at Gabe, "Why? What are you thinking?"

"What if we went with you to get your pelts back?" asked Gabe, grinning.

"You would do that?" replied Francois, surprised.

"If you want. I'd hate to see you lose a whole season of pelts on account of some young bucks trying to prove themselves." He thought a moment, then asked, "Do you have a family?"

"I have a woman that waits for me. She is Algonquin."

Gabe nodded, looked at Ezra, "What do you say?"

"Would it make any difference? You're just bound and determined to get us into trouble. I'd like to go a week, maybe two, that you didn't get us into something!" declared Ezra, rising to gear up the horses, mumbling to himself all the way.

"I was camped in that draw, yonder, and they took off to the southwest toward them buttes," Francois pointed to a series of rolling hills, ridges, and knobby buttes that rose from the grassland. "I'm thinkin' they'd be on the far side of that big one." He pointed to the tracks they followed, "They're heading direct to that." He looked around and motioned for them to follow as he urged his mount to a trot and pointed the hammer head toward the shoulder of the big butte.

Francois slowed to a walk, and carefully picked his route among some juniper and cedar. He lifted his hand to stop them, stepped down and walked to Gabe's side, looking up at the still mounted man. He pointed to the far slope of the shoulder, "I'm certain they are just beyond here. I will go up and look, if I signal you from there, you and Ezra go yonder, leave your horses and work behind the ridge." Gabe nodded and watched the skinny Frenchman climb the rise.

They had already discussed their strategy and both Ezra and Gabe were grinning at the planned assault. They would do their best not to kill anyone, which would be a change and a challenge, but they wanted to retrieve Francois' pelts. He turned back and signaled the two. Gabe looked at Ezra, "Alright, let's go."

They tethered their horses to a juniper and started up the slope. They moved apart, ready to set the plan into action. As they peered over the edge, they saw Francois was right. The dozen young men were dancing about with colored cloth, a few were fighting over a pouch that held brass and nickel buttons, another was stretched out and dipping his fingers in a small bag of sugar and licking the sweet stuff off. Suddenly, Francois came off the hill on his hammer head horse, shouting as he fired his pistol into the air.

The Arapaho jumped as one, some running for their horses, others shouting at them and grabbing for their weapons. Gabe and Ezra stood and fired their pistols into the air, shouting and screaming. Gabe snatched up his Ferguson and fired into the midst of the raiders, hitting the pouch of buttons and scattering them far and wide. The young bucks were startled by the additional shooters and when Gabe and Ezra fired again and again, they were certain there were many coming against them. Those that had been ready to fight, ran for their horses and swung aboard on the run. Gabe sent another shot at their heels, speeding them on their way.

Both Gabe and Ezra dropped to their heels, laughing, and pointing at the fleeing Arapaho. Francois sat aboard his ugly roan, shaking his fist at the fleeing warriors, then looked up at Gabe and Ezra, motioning them to come down and join him. They helped him gather up his pelts and trade goods, loaded them on the three packhorses that remained tethered where the Arapaho had tied them, and started back to their camp.

31 / Mountains

The rest of the day was spent learning from Francois. His experience in the wilderness and mountains was a gold mine for the two friends to quarry nuggets of knowledge. He helped them with the drying racks, showed the ways to cut the meat to make better strips for pemmican. Francois shared recipes for pemmican and told of many plants and herbs that grew wild and could be used for everything from food to medicine. He drew maps in the dirt and quizzed them on landmarks and terrain afterwards.

If Francois had been willing, the men would have spent a week and more with him to garner all the wilderness knowledge they could, but he was bound for home and his way of life as a *coureur des bois*. He was a *Metis* and they had become known as great buffalo hunters and makers of pemmican and more for the many trappers and traders of the Hudson's Bay Company. It was late afternoon on the second day as they were packing away the smoked meat that he turned to them,

"You are wise to travel at night whenever possible. Many of the tribes do not leave their villages at night, they see no purpose. They cannot hunt in the dark and to fight at night is unnecessary and deadly. They will defend themselves and pursue their enemies at any time. Do not underestimate them, they are great warriors."

"So, you're leaving us then?" asked Gabe, watching the man secure the packs of pelts on the horses.

"Oui, my woman misses me, and I must take my pelts to St. Louis. I will sell them and return to my family. I have two growing sons, Jacques and Joseph, that require much."

Gabe stepped closer, "Francois, we are grateful for your wisdom and for sharing with us, you have been a godsend."

"Ahh, my friend, it is you and Ezra that have been the blessing to me. Without you, I would return to my family empty-handed, and my woman, she would not like that!" he chuckled as he thought of his family. It had been almost two years since he had been home and he was anxious to see them.

"We are grateful for your directions about the mountains. We are all the more anxious to see the Rockies and with your guidance, I'm sure we will," added Ezra. The men shook hands, then hugged one another, slapping each other on the back and stepping back. Francois swung aboard, nodded to his new friends, and rode his horse away through the trees.

Gabe and Ezra looked to one another and turned to gear up their horses. Dusk was dropping its curtain as they crossed the river and walked up the west bank to start across the

flatlands. The cicadas were tuning up and a lonesome coyote
cleared his throat and the sounds of the prairie accompanied
the two men as they started northwest, keeping the North
Platte River off their right shoulder, and the north star high
above.

The big moon pushed its way across the starry sky, waded
through the milky-way, and hung lazily overhead when they
stopped for a breather for the horses. They loosened cinches,
led the horses to water in a chuckling stream, and sat back
to let them graze on the blue gramma grass. The men sat on
a flat boulder beneath a rim rock lined mesa and listened to
the night sounds. The coo-coo that ended in a grunt came
from some burrowing owls, and the high-pitched scream
with a drawn-out boom was the sound of the nighthawk. In
the distance a coyote lifted his mating howl to the emptiness,
barking an invitation at the end, waited a few moments and
sounded off again.

They pushed on, hoping to reach the point described by
Francois where the rim-rock mesas overlooked the river and
see the view he described as going on forever. He told them
to take the smaller river that came directly from the west and
met the North Platte. It was just after midnight when they
came to the confluence and turned west to follow the south
edge of the smaller river. The terrain had taken a change,
instead of low rolling hills and endless grass land, now there
were hills, ridges and mesas dotted with juniper and piñon.
Sage brush and cactus were abundant and buffalo grass and
bunch grass offered refuge for rabbits and field mice. Gabe

and Ezra topped a small rise and reined up when the flats before them were marked with mounds of dirt, furrows showing in the middle of the mounds.

Gabe looked to Ezra, "This must be what Francois called a prairie dog village. We best go around it, he said it's a good place for a horse to break a leg."

"Wouldn't want that!" replied Ezra, tugging on the lead rope of his pack horse.

The moon was well past mid sky when the grey light of early morning painted the backs of the riders. Gabe turned back to look as the brilliant pinks and muted golds filled the sky. He nodded as he turned, "Take a look behind you! Tell me that ain't plum pretty!"

"Ummhumm," responded Ezra. "God knows how to start a day, don't He?"

Gabe chuckled, then looked to the west, reined up and paused as he breathed deep. "And lookee there!" He stared in the distance, seeing the morning sun paint the tips of a trio of mountains, one standing head and shoulders above the others. The granite peak blossomed with gold as the light slipped slowly down its timber covered chest. Ezra had stopped beside his friend and stared with equal incredulity and wonder.

"Moonlight and Mountains, can it get any better?" said Gabe, both hands resting on the pommel of his saddle.

Ezra did not respond, but sat in quiet wonder, enjoying the spectacle before him. He turned to his friend, "Didn't Francois say these were just a sampling of what lies beyond?"

"Ummhumm. He said if we cross over these, then we'll see some real mountains."

"If it's alright with you, I'd just as soon find us a camp and get some food and sleep before we do that. I don't think my system can handle much more," suggested Ezra.

Gabe looked at his friend, "Is that all you ever think of, eatin' and sleepin'?"

"No, sometimes its sleepin' and eatin'," chuckled Ezra, turning his horse toward a cluster of juniper that sat on the bank of a chuckling stream. He knew this was where he would lay his head, after he filled his belly.

Away from the draw that held the small stream and the camp of the two friends, sitting atop a rim-rock mesa less than five hundred yards away, a handful of Arapaho warriors watched the visitors make their camp. The leader, also known as the war chief, was Black Eagle. The warriors looked to the leader and she said, "Leave them. We go for buffalo and our people are hungry. These will not go far, and we will return when our bellies are full."

A LOOK AT: MOONLIGHT AND MOUN-TAINS (STONECROFT SAGA 4)

AUTHOR OF THE BEST-SELLING ROCKY MOUNTAIN SAINT SERIES, B.N. RUNDELL, TAKES US ON AN EPIC JOURNEY IN BOOK FOUR OF THE STONECROFT SAGA.

Louisiana Territory had been the exclusive domain of Hudson's Bay Company and the North West Company, seeking to fill their larders with the riches of the uncharted wilderness. But into that territory came two friends, determined to explore and learn about this vast land, land that had seldom if ever had the footprint of a white man.

With their journey already taking them through the lands of the Shawnee, Osage, Pawnee, Omaha and more, they have finally come within sight of the Rocky Mountains, but their way is blocked by the Plains tribes of Arapaho, Ute, Shoshoni, Crow and others.

The challenges of the wilderness never cease, and each day brings unknown dangers and death dealing conflicts, and they are forced to find their way in the unknown wilderness...

AVAILABLE IN APRIL 2020

ABOUT THE AUTHOR

Born and raised in Colorado into a family of ranchers and cowboys, B.N. Rundell is the youngest of seven sons. Juggling bull riding, skiing, and high school, graduation was a launching pad for a hitch in the Army Paratroopers. After the army, he finished his college education in Springfield, MO, and together with his wife and growing family, entered the ministry as a Baptist preacher.

Together, B.N. and Dawn raised four girls that are now married and have made them proud grandparents. With many years as a successful pastor and educator, he retired from the ministry and followed in the footsteps of his entrepreneurial father and started a successful insurance agency, which is now in the hands of his trusted nephew. He has also been a successful audiobook narrator and has recorded many books for several award-winning authors. Now finally realizing his life-long dream, B.N. has turned his efforts to writing a variety of books, from children's picture books and young adult adventure books, to the historical fiction and western genres.

Printed in Great Britain
by Amazon